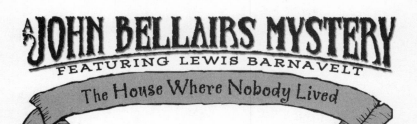

A JOHN BELLAIRS MYSTERY

FEATURING LEWIS BARNAVELT

The House Where Nobody Lived

A JOHN BELLAIRS MYSTERY
FEATURING LEWIS BARNAVELT
The House Where Nobody Lived

BRAD STRICKLAND

By Brad Strickland
(based on John Bellairs's characters)

The House Where Nobody Lived
The Whistle, the Grave, and the Ghost
The Tower at the End of the World
The Beast under the Wizard's Bridge
The Wrath of the Grinning Ghost
The Specter from the Magician's Museum
The Bell, the Book, and the Spellbinder
The Hand of the Necromancer

Books by John Bellairs
Completed by Brad Strickland

The Doom of the Haunted Opera
The Drum, the Doll, and the Zombie
The Vengeance of the Witch-Finder
The Ghost in the Mirror

Books by John Bellairs

The Mansion in the Mist
The Secret of the Underground Room
The Chessmen of Doom
The Trolley to Yesterday
The Lamp from the Warlock's Tomb
The Eyes of the Killer Robot
The Revenge of the Wizard's Ghost
The Spell of the Sorcerer's Skull
The Dark Secret of Weatherend
The Mummy, the Will, and the Crypt
The Curse of the Blue Figurine
The Treasure of Alpheus Winterborn
The Letter, the Witch, and the Ring
The Figure in the Shadows
The House with a Clock in Its Walls

DIAL BOOKS FOR YOUNG READERS
A division of Penguin Young Readers Group
Published by The Penguin Group
Penguin Group (USA) Inc.,
375 Hudson Street, New York, NY 10014, U.S.A.
Penguin Group (Canada), 90 Eglinton Avenue East, Suite 700,
Toronto, Ontario, Canada M4P 2Y3
(a division of Pearson Penguin Canada Inc.)
Penguin Books Ltd, 80 Strand, London WC2R 0RL, England
Penguin Ireland, 25 St. Stephen's Green, Dublin 2, Ireland
(a division of Penguin Books Ltd)
Penguin Group (Australia), 250 Camberwell Road,
Camberwell, Victoria 3124, Australia
(a division of Pearson Australia Group Pty Ltd)
Penguin Books India Pvt Ltd, 11 Community Centre, Panchsheel Park,
New Delhi - 110 017, India
Penguin Group (NZ), Cnr Airborne and Rosedale Roads,
Albany, Auckland 1310, New Zealand
(a division of Pearson New Zealand Ltd)
Penguin Books (South Africa) (Pty) Ltd, 24 Sturdee Avenue,
Rosebank, Johannesburg 2196, South Africa
Penguin Books Ltd, Registered Offices: 80 Strand,
London WC2R 0RL, England

Book design by Jasmin Rubero
Text set in Cg Cloister
Printed in the U.S.A.
1 3 5 7 9 10 8 6 4 2
Library of Congress Cataloging-in-Publication Data
Strickland, Brad.
The house where nobody lived / by Brad Strickland.
p. cm.
"A John Bellairs mystery featuring Lewis Barnavelt."
Summary: Twelve-year-old Lewis and his best friend Rose Rita investigate
a strange old house in their home town and discover
that they may be dealing with powerful ancient Hawaiian spirits.
ISBN 0-8037-3148-5
[1. Magic—Fiction. 2. Supernatural—Fiction. 3. Wizards—Fiction.] I. Title.
PZ7.S916703Ho 2006
[Fic]—dc22
2006001673

For Amy, my daughter,
who always sees the magic

—B.S.

CHAPTER 1

O N A BLISTERING SUMMER day, a boy and a girl were walking north on a weedy path near a highway in Michigan. The boy, whose name was Lewis Barnavelt, was puffing and sweating as he struggled to keep up with the girl. "It's too hot for hiking," Lewis complained. "Let's go back home and play checkers or something."

"Oh, don't be silly. You need to explore!" returned the girl, whose name was Rose Rita Pottinger. She tossed her long, straight black hair and grinned back at him. "Besides, this isn't a hike. It's a stroll! C'mon, Lewis!" She strode along in front of him, swinging a stick and beheading tall burdock weeds and gangly dandelions as if they were enemy knights.

This was the way Lewis was later to remember it

all beginning. At that time, he was just eleven years old and still fairly new in town. A little more than a year earlier, both of his parents had died in an awful car crash, and then the previous August, Lewis had come from Wisconsin to live with his uncle Jonathan in a wonderful old mansion at 100 High Street in New Zebedee, Michigan.

That first year had been hard. Lewis was overweight, clumsy at sports, and timid, and worst of all, he found it hard to make friends. True, some wonderful things happened. For one thing, he discovered that his cheerful, pot-bellied, red-bearded uncle Jonathan was a sorcerer, and not simply a conjurer who could do card tricks and pretend to pluck quarters from your ears, but a real magician who could wave his cane and summon up wonderfully lifelike three-dimensional illusions.

And their next-door neighbor, a retired schoolteacher named Florence Zimmermann, wasn't just a friendly, wrinkly-faced lady who loved to dress all in purple and cook delicious meals for Uncle Jonathan and Lewis, but she was also a *maga,* which Uncle Jonathan explained was just a fancy word for "witch." As Lewis soon learned, Mrs. Zimmermann wasn't an evil witch, but a good and kindly one, and her magic was even more powerful than Uncle Jonathan's.

In a way, the best surprise of all was when Lewis met a new friend, the tall, dark-haired, homely girl named Rose Rita Pottinger, who was something of a tomboy and who knew the names of all kinds of cannons, from sakers to demi-culverins, from minions to falconets. Rose Rita took Lewis under her wing and, in the summer of his first full year in New Zebedee, she dragged him along on long walks around the area, pointing out this and that and reeling off the history of things like the stone Civil War Memorial and the round fountain in the center of town.

Lewis usually complained that after these walks his legs ached and his heels were blistered, but in fact he enjoyed listening to Rose Rita, who loved to talk about things she found interesting. He began to be interested too, and despite his grumbling, he was always secretly glad when Rose Rita turned up and suggested some new expedition.

On that particular sweltering July day they had hiked out north of town, where the road ran through woods before it reached farmland rich and green with fragrant corn. Rose Rita, dressed in a red T-shirt and jeans, was chopping off the heads of weeds with her stick, occasionally shouting, "Ha! Have at thee, varlet!" while Lewis plodded along behind her, with sweat pouring down his face. He flinched a little every time the stick chopped its way through another dandelion. Suddenly Rose Rita stopped dead in her tracks, and Lewis nearly blundered right into her. "That's funny," said Rose Rita in a thoughtful voice as Lewis staggered to a halt.

"What's funny?" asked Lewis, fishing a crumpled

handkerchief from the pocket of his brown corduroy pants and swabbing his dripping face. "Other than the fact that I'm about to have heatstroke?"

Rose Rita raised her stick to point dramatically off to the left. "That crooked old lane," she said. "I don't think I've ever explored it."

Lewis gave the overgrown path a dubious look. The lane was barely a path at all, more an overgrown patch of treeless ground twisting and turning between the dark woods. "Not much there to look at," he grunted. "If we're going to explore, let's walk on the way we're going. You've got tons of weeds you haven't killed yet."

"Come on," replied Rose Rita, raising her stick high overhead, like a cavalry officer urging his men onward with drawn sword. "We have met the enemy and he is ours! Full speed ahead! You may fire when ready, Gridley!" With that, she plunged away from the path beside the road and headed down the overgrown lane, between two thick stands of butternut and oak trees.

Lewis followed, but he got a creepy feeling in his stomach. Though the sun shone bright on the tall green weeds overgrowing the lane, deep shadows pooled like spilled ink beneath the trees. Anything could lurk there, snakes or wild animals. Lewis told himself to get a grip and reminded himself that they weren't really far from home. This wasn't the deep woods or anything, just a patch of trees on the outskirts of town. If he got too scared, he could probably run back to 100 High Street in less than five minutes. Rose Rita had courage to spare, though, and maybe some of it soaked into him. He swallowed hard and in his waddling trot he closed the distance until he was right behind Rose Rita again. "This is spooky," he complained as they walked along, the tall grass and weeds swacking against his pant legs. "I don't like the way the trees grow so close."

"It's like a real jungle," agreed Rose Rita. "You might meet a tyrannosaur in here, or a giant anaconda, or maybe a grizzly or two. I wonder where this lane goes. It twists and turns too much to ever have been a regular street."

"Maybe it was—" began Lewis. He broke off and exclaimed, "There's a house."

It was the most peculiar one he had ever seen. It stood in a patch of chest-high weeds and looked as out of place as a beached ocean liner. The main part of the building stretched out long, with a three-story-tall veranda running around it, the overhanging roof so wide that it cast everything under it in deep shade. Right in the center of the structure rose a sort of squarish tower yet another story tall, with a strange, curving, sharply peaked roof over an open platform at least forty feet off the ground. The house looked abandoned, though oddly undamaged. Its walls had been painted in shades of pale lime-green and pink and white.

"It looks Chinese," muttered Lewis.

Rose Rita shook her head in an absentminded sort of way. "I don't think so. I mean, that tower looks a little bit like a pagoda, but not really. But what I can't figure out is why I've never heard of this place. My folks and I must've driven past that lane about a zillion times, but this is the first time I ever noticed it. Nobody's lived here for years."

"What makes you say that?" asked Lewis in an uneasy voice. He had just been imagining some crazy old geezer who would come roaring out of the house, carrying a shotgun, screaming his head off about trespassers.

"Elementary, Watson," Rose Rita shot back. "The lane must have been the driveway to this place. But you saw how overgrown it was with horsetail and witchgrass and even butternut saplings. Nobody's driven a car, or even a horse and buggy, down this way in ages. Come on, let's take a closer look."

Despite the heat, Lewis felt a little cold knot tie itself in his stomach. It was his curse to be not only timid, but also imaginative. He could picture the worst disasters in his mind, and once he had dreamed them up, it was almost as if they were all about to come true. "What if somebody's in there?"

"Does it look like there's anyone inside?"

"N-no," agreed Lewis reluctantly. "But it's not polite to go barging into somebody's house."

"We're not going *inside,*" said Rose Rita. "We're just going *closer,* that's all."

They edged forward. Years of rain and sun and wind had eroded the ground close to the house, so that a gully ran alongside the veranda, where rain had sheeted off and carved out a miniature ravine. They walked along the edge, with Rose Rita peering down through her round black-rimmed spectacles. She suddenly stooped and with a triumphant cry she picked up something white from the dirt. She thumbed some soil off and then held it up so that Lewis could see it. "An arrowhead?" he asked.

"Just the tip of one. You can have this one," she said, dropping it into his palm. "I've found about a thousand of them."

Lewis turned the small white chip over and over. A little longer than his thumbnail, it felt strangely smooth and rounded, not like stone at all. The edges, however, were sharp and serrated. He never found things like this. He and Rose Rita could be sauntering along the street, and she would bend down and pick up a fifty-cent piece that he had walked right past. He couldn't figure out why he missed things like that, though Rose Rita insisted he just had to teach himself to be more observant. He carefully dropped the broken arrowhead into his shirt pocket.

"Funny," Rose Rita said quietly. They had taken a long step across the wash-out and had stopped just in front of the wide steps that ran up to the veranda.

"I wonder what happened to this place. It must have been abandoned years ago, but the paint isn't all scabby and flaky. The windows are dirty, but none of them are broken, and you know how the other kids are when they come across an empty building. They pick up a few rocks, and there go the windows."

"I don't like this place," insisted Lewis.

"I'm going up on the porch."

"No, don't." Lewis swallowed hard. "It—it doesn't feel right. It, uh, it could be some kind of a trap."

Rose Rita tilted her head, her dark hair swinging around her face. "You sound like you think we're in an episode of *Lights Out*." That was a horror show on the radio. It came on late at night, and Lewis never listened to it, because if he heard even a little part of it, his dreams shambled with living mummies, shrieked with vicious bats, and dripped with a slow ooze of blood.

"I just don't want to go up there," muttered Lewis, ashamed of his own timidity.

"Then stay here," returned Rose Rita, dropping her stick.

Lewis tried to gulp down the pounding lump in his throat as Rose Rita tested the steps one at a time, placing her feet carefully. "Seems to be sturdy enough," she said. She walked across the veranda, and Lewis could hear the creaking of the boards beneath her feet. "Almost looks as if someone cleaned this from time to time," she reported. "I mean, there are a few dead leaves here and there, but not the kind of mess you'd expect." She made her way over to one of a number of tall, narrow windows and tried to gaze inside, cupping her hands up beside her eyes and leaning close. "Can't see a thing—"

From somewhere close, so loud that it made Lewis's heart thud, a drum boomed once.

CHAPTER 2

T HE UNEXPECTED NOISE MADE both of
them jump, and Rose Rita yelped in alarm. She
leaped away from the window and sprang down from
the veranda without even touching the steps. Lewis
thought he was about to choke on his own thud-
ding heart. The first echoing boom had been the
loudest, but now he heard an insistent, angry drumming, coming from somewhere inside the mysterious
house, a rhythm that seemed to say: "Doom-doom-
doom-doom-doom."

Rose Rita stopped beside him and grabbed the stick
she had tossed aside. "What in the world is that?"

"Somebody inside," said Lewis in a voice that
sounded as if someone were smothering him. "My
gosh, let's go."

Rose Rita shook her head. "Maybe it's animals or something." She raised her voice and yelled, "Hey!"

Sudden silence fell, even more frightening to Lewis than the drumming sound. Now it seemed to him as though the house were watching them, like a huge cat staring at a couple of mice that had ventured almost within reach. "Let's go," he groaned again.

"Maybe rats in the walls?" asked Rose Rita. "Or squirrels up in the attic?"

"I—don't—care," insisted Lewis doggedly. "Let's get out of here. I'm going. Now."

"Okay, okay," said Rose Rita. "Keep your hair on your head."

They turned and headed back down the twisting lane, Lewis taking the lead and walking so fast that Rose Rita had to hurry to keep up. At first everything was silent, but after a dozen steps or so, Lewis heard it again, that ominous rhythm that sounded as though someone were pounding on a drum off in the distance. Rose Rita gave no sign that she had heard it, though, and he was just as happy not to mention it. Somehow the shadows under the trees had grown even murkier, and from time to time Lewis could have sworn that someone—a whole group of people, in fact—was walking alongside them, dodging behind the trees, a row of grim figures in single file, keeping pace with the two kids. He had to force himself to look directly at them, and when he did, they vanished, melting into the green gloom beneath the trees.

The lane met the path near the highway, and as Lewis and Rose Rita stepped out onto the weedy shoulder, a second boom hit, so loud that Lewis flinched, feeling his knees give way, and Rose Rita yipped again.

But this time it was thunder. A purplish black cloud had rolled up from the west, and the two of them raced it back to 100 High Street, arriving just before the first huge drops of rain plopped down. The two of them hurried through the door, and behind them the storm battered the porch as the house across the street vanished behind a gray downpour.

"Here you are," said Lewis's red-bearded uncle Jonathan, coming out of the kitchen. "Mrs. Zimmermann and I were just about to set out to find you two. Lucky you got home when you did. Florence," he said, raising his voice, "the stray sheep have returned to the fold, or to fold up, or something. I'd better give Rose Rita's folks a call."

In stormy weather, Uncle Jonathan never stayed on the phone long, because he always was afraid that lightning might run in on the lines and fry him, or so he said, but he did make a quick call to Mrs. Pottinger. When he hung up the phone, he said, "Your mother says to stay put until this blows over, Rose Rita, and that means you can sample some of Frizzy Wig's best walnut-fudge brownies."

Lewis gave a little grin. His uncle and Mrs. Zimmermann teased each other by thinking up insulting nicknames, but they were good-natured about it. Lewis felt the tension easing out of him as they sat around the kitchen table. The rain soon slackened to a steady, gentle shower, and Mrs. Zimmermann, wearing one of her baggy purple dresses, cheerfully pulled a pan of delicious, chocolatey, gooey brownies from the oven. They all had some of the warm bars with big glasses of cold milk, and before long Lewis's heart had stopped feeling as if it were a cornered animal trying to batter its way out of a trap.

It lurched again, though, when Rose Rita suddenly asked, "Mrs. Zimmermann, what is that strange old house north of town, about half a mile off the highway?"

Mrs. Zimmermann's spectacles suddenly gleamed as she turned her head toward Rose Rita. Her white eyebrows rose in surprise, but her eyes narrowed. "Have you two been exploring that dangerous old place?" she demanded, her voice surprisingly sharp.

"Well, not exactly," said Rose Rita. "But we saw it."

Mrs. Zimmermann touched her chin thoughtfully with her right index finger. "Hmm. What do you think, Weird Beard? Should we tell them?"

Uncle Jonathan shrugged. "I don't think it's any great secret. Funny how people forget about the Hawaii House, though."

"The what?" asked Lewis.

"It's called the Hawaii House," Uncle Jonathan repeated. "And that's because it was built by a sea captain who settled down here in the middle of Michigan about, oh, seventy-five years ago or so, a few years after the Civil War. What was his name, Florence?"

"Chadwick," returned Mrs. Zimmermann at once. "Captain Abediah Chadwick, originally of Boston. He was the captain of a ship that took representatives of the United States government from San Francisco to the Sandwich Islands in the year 1869."

"It was a voyage of exploration," explained Uncle Jonathan. "They wanted to see if the Sandwich Islands were ham on rye or Swiss cheese on whole wheat."

Mrs. Zimmermann snorted. "As Frazzle Face very well knows, the Sandwich Islands were given that name by Captain James Cook, in honor of John Montagu, the Earl of Sandwich. Later, though, they came to be called the Hawaiian Islands. Anyway, Captain Chadwick spent three years there, and during that time he met a beautiful young Hawaiian princess, or so the stories say. He was about fifty, and she was less than half his age. Her people tried to prevent them from getting together, but just like in a fairy tale, she fell in love with Abediah Chadwick and he with her, and the princess ran away with him. He married her at sea, and when he got back to the United States, he decided to take her as far away from the ocean as he could. They wound up here in Michigan."

"Old Chadwick sold his shipping business and retired with a fortune," put in Uncle Jonathan. "He built his bride a magnificent house just outside of town, with lots of land around it. He wanted it to remind her of her home islands, so it was unlike any other house around here. It looked like a mansion that might be owned by a rich Hawaiian pineapple rancher."

Lewis wasn't sure that pineapples were grown on ranches, but before he could ask, Rose Rita broke in with a question: "Did they live happily ever after?"

Uncle Jonathan and Mrs. Zimmermann exchanged a long look, and Uncle Jonathan tugged uneasily at his beard. "Well—no."

"We don't know that," said Mrs. Zimmerman in a grim voice. "All we know is what happened. Chadwick hired a big staff of servants to help run that place—three maids and a butler, as well as a gardener and a cook. They all had rooms in the mansion. But in 1875 or 1876—I don't remember which, but they say it was exactly one year to the day after the house was finished—well, they all died, all in one night."

"What?" Rose Rita sat up straight. "Did he go crazy and kill them, or—"

Uncle Jonathan raised his hand. "No, no, and no. They all just—died. I'm not going to go into details, because then Lewis would have the heebie-jeebies for a month, but I will say that all of the people in the house seemed to be perfectly sound except for the fact that they weren't breathing. This was during a cold winter, and one of the victims, Abediah Chadwick himself, seemed to have frozen to death, but no one knows what happened to the others. People thought it might have been some weird disease, but if it was, no one else ever caught it."

"But you can imagine how people in New Zebedee reacted to the terrible news," said Mrs. Zimmermann. "One of Abediah Chadwick's relatives out in New England inherited the house. He tried to rent it out, but no one would ever stay in the place because of what happened. Eventually he sold it, very cheaply, to some real estate company or other. Years later they fixed it up by wiring it for electricity and adding modern plumbing, but even so they could never interest anyone around here in buying the place. Years passed and the For Sale signs rotted and fell apart and the company simply stopped trying to sell or rent the old place. So it just stands out there, with quite a forest growing around it now. I expect it's in pretty bad repair."

"No," said Rose Rita. "That's the funny part. It doesn't look bad at all. Just empty."

"Well," said Uncle Jonathan, "be that as it may, it's no place to go prowling around. It still belongs to some real estate company or other, and companies can be very touchy about little things like trespassing.

Promise me that you two won't go near it again."

"I promise," Lewis said fervently.

It took Rose Rita a couple of minutes, but finally she gave her word too.

It was a promise that both of them kept for months, and then for years. At first Rose Rita would mention the old house every once in a while, but in time other things came along to occupy them. Eventually Lewis all but forgot about the isolated building, the drumming sound, and the ghastly story of how everyone in the Hawaii House had died all in one night.

And then, a long time later, when Lewis was over thirteen, something happened.

CHAPTER 3

THE LEWIS BARNAVELT WHO started school that year in the 1950s was not only older, but also a little braver and a little more confident. In the years since they had first seen the Hawaii House, Lewis and Rose Rita had shared some pretty amazing adventures. Rose Rita had taught Lewis to play a fair game of baseball. She was a real baseball fiend, not only a good pitcher and batter, but a walking encyclopedia of facts and figures about the game. After Uncle Jonathan treated Lewis to a long summer vacation in Europe, where they walked for miles at a stretch and where the strange food did not appeal to his appetite, Lewis had lost some weight. He still was heavyset, though not as chubby as he had once been. At least, for a long time no one, not even the annoying little kids, had yelled the insulting rhyme at him:

Fatty, fatty, two by four,

Can't get through the kitchen door!

Oh, it was true that Lewis was still clumsy on the baseball field and so timid that he didn't dare play football for fear of getting hurt. He still loved to read piles of books about adventures in strange, far-away places. And he still fretted when other kids sometimes teased him about being too smart for his own good or called him "teacher's pet." Still, he had finally decided that he would never be a real athlete, and now he didn't worry about that anymore. He was becoming far more interested in things like astronomy than sports, anyway.

When school started that year, Lewis learned that for the first time he would be changing classes. Up until then, he had been with one or maybe two teachers all day, first the nuns at the Catholic school and then later the teachers at the public school. Beginning on the day after Labor Day, however, Lewis would now report to Mr. Beemuth's homeroom. After that, he would have to go to Mrs. Zane's English class, then to Mr. Furling's math class, and so on, ending up back with Mr. Beemuth for science in the afternoon. Rose Rita was in just two classes with him, which threw Lewis into the dumps.

"I don't like this crazy old schedule," he fretted to Rose Rita at lunch on the first day. "I don't know if I'll ever be able to remember where my classes are and when they start. I'll probably flunk out of school, and then I'll have to go be a garbage man and ride on that stinky truck with Skunky Stevenson!"

Rose Rita was drinking milk, and she laughed so suddenly that some of it shot out her nose. "Stop it! Ow!" she complained, reaching for a napkin. "Look, Lewis, if you can remember the names of Jupiter's moons, and when Venus transits the sun and the whatzis and whosis of Mars—"

"Right ascension and declination," Lewis said. "It isn't that hard—"

Rose Rita carried right on: "—then you certainly can remember when to go to English and so on. What made you think of Skunky, anyway?"

Lewis shrugged. Skunky wasn't the man's real name, of course. In fact, he had what Uncle Jonathan called a three-barreled name: Potsworth Farmer Stevenson the Fourth. He was a squatty, red-faced, bleary-eyed man with a frost of gray hair around his lumpy bald head, and he always seemed about a beat and a half behind everyone around him. His family had been rich, but Potsworth Farmer Stevenson the Fourth had lost all the money he had inherited. People felt sorry for him, and at last the town had hired him to be the assistant sanitation man, which meant he got bossed around by foul-mouthed old Jute Feasel as he drove the clanking, battered garbage truck through the streets of New Zebedee.

To Lewis, Skunky Stevenson represented the terrible things that could happen to a person, and the kind of things that he sometimes feared might happen to him. He was about to explain this to Rose Rita when he heard a commotion behind him. He turned away from his unappealing lunch of soggy, cold fish sticks, runny but lumpy mashed potatoes, and wilted green beans to see who was laughing behind him.

He saw a skinny, miserable-looking boy about his own age standing near a table, holding a tray of food. The four boys already sitting at the table were talking to the kid with the tray, but they sounded anything but friendly. "G-g-g-go s-s-s-sit s-s-s-s-omewhere else, you baby," mocked Curt Schellmacher, the shortest of the four boys, in an exaggerated stammer.

"He's gonna cry," said big Jimmy Taubman, while the others laughed in a nasty way.

"Great," growled Rose Rita, starting to get up from the table. "I'd better straighten this out."

"Don't make it worse on him," warned Lewis. Instead of making a big deal of it, Lewis just motioned to the standing boy, and with a look of relief in his eyes, the new kid noticed and hurried toward them. Mike Dugan, another of the boys at the table, stuck out his big black P.F. Flyers sneaker and tripped him, and the new kid went sprawling, milk, mashed potatoes, and fish sticks splattering everywhere.

Lewis jumped up, and he and Rose Rita helped the poor guy get to his feet as Mrs. Thayer, a plump, kind, gray-haired lunchroom lady, hurried over with a towel. "My goodness!" she said. "What happened?"

The boy's thin face turned so red, it was nearly purple. "T-t-t-tripped," he stammered. "Muh-my f-fault."

Rose Rita's eyes flashed in surprise and anger. Lewis saw her glare toward the four boys who had been teasing the victim, and he gave a warning shake of his head. Lewis knew what it was like to be bullied and browbeaten, and Rose Rita didn't. Mrs. Thayer swabbed potatoes off the boy's red plaid flannel shirt, then helped him pick up his tray, plate, and tableware. "You sit down," she said in a motherly way. "I'll bring you something to eat."

As she hurried away with the tray and the ruins of the lunch, the boy slid gratefully into the empty seat beside Lewis. He clenched his fists on top of the table and stared at them, his blue eyes red-rimmed and shiny with tears.

"Those guys are jerks," Lewis said quietly. "Don't let them know they got to you, or it will never end."

"Most of the kids here aren't like that," put in Rose Rita. "Most of us have a little sense."

Lewis scooped up a little of his mashed potatoes on a fork and let it gloop off in a runny, stringy blob. "Anyway, they were actually doing you a favor."

The boy tried to smile, but it was the most miserable-looking smile Lewis had ever seen. Mrs.

Thayer returned with a little glass bottle of milk, a peanut butter and jelly sandwich, and an apple. "Here you are, dear," she said. "Maybe this will hold you. I'm sorry, but we're all out of fish sticks."

When she had left, Lewis said, "Wow, you got actual food. Maybe tomorrow I can get those guys to trip me." He held out his hand. "I'm Lewis Barnavelt. This is my friend Rose Rita Pottinger. Welcome to the wonderful world of New Zebedee public school!"

The boy seemed too shy to shake Lewis's hand. "I'm Duh-D-Duh-" he started, his face turning all red again. "Muh-my nuh-name is, is, is, Duh-David. David Kuh-Keller," he finished in a strained voice.

"Better hurry and eat," said Rose Rita, looking at her watch. "We have to get to the next class in seven minutes and sixteen seconds."

David pulled the little round paper lid off his bottle of milk and took a gulp. "I cuh-c-can't tuh-talk vuh-v-very good," he confessed.

Lewis felt the terrible tension that the effort had cost David, and he felt sorry for the kid. "That's okay," he said. "Everybody can't do something. Rose Rita's right, though. You don't have much time. You'd better eat up unless you want your stomach to growl in your next class."

David nodded and hastily munched his way through the peanut butter and grape jelly sandwich. He offered the apple silently to Lewis.

"No, thanks," Lewis said, making a face. "I already had the delicious and nutritious lime Jell-O cube with a grape floating in the middle. You eat the apple."

"I wuh-wanted to th-thank you," David said in a low voice. "Everybody else makes fuh-fun of muh-me."

Rose Rita smiled. She would never be a great beauty, but Lewis had often thought that no one had a better face for smiling than Rose Rita. "That's all right, David," she said. "Listen, the other girls call me Beanpole and Four Eyes, and people used to call Lewis Tubby and—"

"Hey," Lewis objected, but he was grinning.

"—and other names," said Rose Rita. "But you know what? He and I decided that the names they call us aren't our problem. They don't really mean anything. Except that the people who call us those things are morons."

David actually chuckled at that. He didn't try to speak again, but just nodded. A moment later, the bell rang, and all the students at lunch trudged off to their next classes.

Lewis and David had history with Mrs. Angdale, who was about the oldest teacher at the school. She was tall and thin, with a big beak of a nose and white hair that she kept in a hard-looking bun at the very back of her head. She always wore black dresses, and before the end of every day, her dresses had streaks and sprinkles of white chalk dust all over them.

Because her eyesight was very bad, Mrs. Angdale wore big, heavy square-rimmed glasses, with lenses so thick, they made her eyes look enormous, like a lizard's eyes. She was also hard of hearing, and she insisted that you answer very loudly when she called the roll.

"Lewis Barnavelt!" she said, staring down at her attendance book.

"Here!" Lewis replied, loud and clear.

"Mary Callandar!"

And so on, until Mrs. Angdale reached "David Keller!"

David's face turned tomato-red, and he struggled to say, "Huh-h-huh-huh—" Some of the other kids started to snicker.

Lewis dropped his voice to a lower pitch and quickly said, "Here!" as if he were performing a ventriloquist's trick. Some of the other kids looked at Lewis in surprise, and Patty Lowan giggled and snorted, but Mrs. Angdale did not appear to hear that. She seemed to assume that David had answered when she called his name, and she never even glanced up from her roll book. "Lawrence Lemon," she said, mispronouncing Larry's name so it sounded like the fruit.

"Le-*mon*," squawked Larry, as Patty guffawed again, but Mrs. Angdale just checked him off and then went on calling out names. David gave Lewis a glance of such pure relief that Lewis wondered if the poor kid had ever had a friend before.

CHAPTER 4

WHEN SCHOOL ENDED, LEWIS met Rose Rita out front. "How was it?" he asked.

She made a face. "Most of it's okay, but I really don't want to take home ec. Maybe I can talk my way into science with you. I don't want to learn how to make clothes and bake cherry pies—I want to be a famous writer someday, not Betty Crocker!"

David came out, lugging a heavy load of books, and he gave them a shy smile as he waved at them. "Walking home?" Lewis asked him.

Shaking his head, David pointed at one of the two yellow school buses parked nearby. Most of the kids in school came from homes within walking distance, but forty or fifty of them lived outside the city limits, out on farms or in one of the little villages close to New Zebedee. "See you tomorrow," Lewis said as David climbed on the bus that took kids to outlying homes that were north and east of town.

He fell into step beside Rose Rita. "Poor guy," he said. "I remember when I was new in town and people made fun of me all the time."

"You were right when you said people like that are idiots," said Rose Rita in a moody voice. Then she brightened up. "You know what? We should show David around, help him learn the ropes."

"That's okay with me," replied Lewis. "But I get the feeling he'd be kind of uncomfortable if we're too obvious about it. The last thing someone wants is people being nice just because they feel sorry for them. I know."

"I don't feel sorry for him," insisted Rose Rita. "Well, I mean I do, but it's not *just* that. He seems like a pretty nice guy. And we're pretty nice too, if I do say it myself. We're not mean, like Woody Mingo, or stuck-up, like Brenda Biggins, anyway. If David wants to hang around with us, at least we'll treat him like a person."

"Sure," agreed Lewis. He thought a minute. "You know, maybe I can invite David to the house for lunch one day. Uncle Jonathan won't mind—at least he won't mind if Mrs. Zimmermann comes over too, and does the cooking. Then maybe you and I could show David around a little."

"Sounds good," said Rose Rita. "How about Saturday?"

"I'll ask."

As Lewis expected, Uncle Jonathan readily agreed. When Lewis explained David's problem, Uncle Jonathan clucked in sympathy. "You know, your dad and I had a friend like that when we were kids," he said. "His name was, let me see . . . Francis. People made fun of him because he stuttered so badly, and Francis was the skinniest, saddest kid you ever laid eyes on. I remember once your dad saw two big kids beating him up. Well, Charlie was three years younger than me, you know, and he was never as big or muscular as I am." Uncle Jonathan's eyes twinkled, because in fact he was rather sloppy and lazy, and Lewis's dad had been the athlete in the family, a star baseball player and a whiz at track. "But Charlie had a lot of spirit for a little guy. Anyway, he waded in, and between them he and Francis decked those two bullies. Francis started to hang around with us, and we got to know him. He was a great kid. We started calling him Frank, and one day Charlie made an amazing discovery. When Frank sang his words instead of talking them, his stutter evaporated! Frank worked on his singing, and you know who he became?"

"Frank Sinatra?" asked Lewis, naming one of the most famous singers he had ever heard of.

Uncle Jonathan shook his head. "Well, no. His name is Frank Gartener. But he became the owner of a fabulous restaurant in Chicago, and now he's so rich that no one cares if he stumbles over his T's and D's!"

Lewis smiled dutifully, but he wasn't sure that singing would help David. In fact, he wasn't sure that anything would.

The next day Lewis asked David if he wanted to come and have lunch at 100 High Street on Saturday. "My uncle can drive me over and we'll pick you up," he said. "Come over about eleven, and then Rose Rita and I will show you around downtown."

Shyly, David said he would ask his folks if it was all right. And the day after, he said it was, except that Uncle Jonathan didn't have to drive out to get him. "M-m-my dad h-has to c-come into t-town anyway," he explained painfully. So they arranged to meet at eleven in front of Heemsoth's Rexall Drug Store, which was right in the middle of the main street through the center of town.

When Saturday morning came, Rose Rita showed up bright and early. Uncle Jonathan was out in the front yard, running the lawn mower around under the chestnut tree to make the ground soft, he said, for the fall leaves that would soon be tumbling down. When Lewis and Rose Rita started out to meet David, Uncle Jonathan paused to mop his face with a big red bandanna and beckoned them over. "Listen," he said, his face shining under his mop of red hair, "maybe it would be best if you two didn't mention you-know-what to David. We don't want him to think he's having lunch with some escapees from the loony bin."

Lewis smiled. "We won't say a word about you or Mrs. Zimmermann knowing magic," he promised.

"Or about the Capharnaum County Magicians Society," added Rose Rita. Oddly enough for such a small area, Capharnaum County and its county seat, New Zebedee, had a big supply of sorcerers, magicians, and wizards, although most people who lived there never even suspected that fact.

It was a warm day for early September, and they were early, so Lewis and Rose Rita sauntered down High Street. The trees that lined it had spread out at the tops over the years, and now it was a little like walking through a green tunnel. They reached Mansion Street, strolled past Rose Rita's house, and then continued down to the center of town. A few cars rattled slowly past, but the streets of town seemed lazy and sleepy, as if Labor Day had put everyone into a light doze. The stores still had Back to School displays in the windows, but not many people were shopping that morning.

At the drugstore, Rose Rita looked at her watch and announced they were eleven minutes and twenty seconds early. "Oh, dry up," said Lewis in a teasing way. "You just like to show off your wristwatch!"

The watch had been a birthday present, and Rose

Rita was very proud of it. She grinned back at Lewis, then stuck out her tongue. "Think it would be okay to have a soda?"

"Maybe a small one," said Lewis.

They sat at the counter and sipped a couple of small Cokes full of crushed ice until their straws made the rackety sound at the end, and just then a black Chevrolet parked in front of the drugstore and David climbed out of the passenger side. Lewis and Rose Rita hurried out, and David introduced the lanky, balding driver of the car as his dad.

Mr. Keller had mild blue eyes behind rimless spectacles. He looked like an older version of David, but he didn't have a stutter. "Hi, Lewis. Hi, Rose Rita," he said with a weary smile. "My name's Ernest Keller. I'm glad David has met a couple of friends. My wife and I have got a million things to do to fix up the house we've bought, and David, well, he gets bored because we're too busy to pay much attention to him. Anyway, have him call me when he's ready to come home, and I'll pick him up here or come over to your house for him. Okay?"

Lewis noticed that David blushed furiously when his dad talked about him, and he noticed too that Mr. Keller talked to him instead of to his son. Mr. Keller went into Corrigan's Hardware, and Lewis, Rose Rita, and David walked back to High Street and up the hill.

"This is our house," said Lewis as he lifted the

looped shoelace that kept the wrought-iron gate closed. He expected some sort of reaction from David, because the house was pretty spectacular, a three-story stone mansion with a tall turret on the front. But David just nodded politely.

Mrs. Zimmermann had prepared a hearty meal of roast beef sandwiches, golden yellow potato salad, crispy-tangy cole slaw, and her own gloriously sour and crunchy dill pickles, all of it washed down with fresh, tart lemonade and last but best, a German chocolate cake that made Lewis sigh with anticipation. "It's supposed to be past picnic season," she announced, "but I say pooh to that! The birds are singing, the sun is shining, and Jonathan has a perfectly good backyard that is going to waste, so we're going to rough it."

They didn't, of course. The backyard was very comfortable, and they sat at a folding table and ate and ate until they were all full. Then Uncle Jonathan took out his harmonica. "David, we have found by scientific experimentation that the best way to digest a meal like that is to have a sing-along. Do you bray like a frightened mule? Can you hit a high C? How about a high W? If all the dogs in the neighborhood howl every time you raise your voice—congratulations! You're just the tenor our little group needs!"

David was giggling at that. Lewis thought he knew what his uncle was up to, though it was true they often sang their heads off just for fun. Mrs.

Zimmermann started a silly song, "The Walloping Window Blind," and David timidly joined in once he learned the chorus. They went on to other songs like "It Ain't Gonna Rain No More" and a sort of jazzy version of "My Bonnie Lies Over the Ocean." Lewis noticed that David hardly stammered or stuttered at all when they were singing.

When they had sung themselves out, Uncle Jonathan stood up and stretched. "This has been a lot of fun," he said. "But now I think Rose Rita and Lewis are eager to take you on a personal tour of beautiful downtown New Zebedee. Come back when you're ready to call it a day, and I'll be glad to pull my old car out of the garage and run you home, David. I'll bet you've never ridden in a Muggins Simoon before!"

"Nuh-n-no, sir," said David happily.

"Very well, then, I will be happy to be your chauffeur."

"O-okay, but it's s-sort of hard to fuh-find," replied David, turning pink as he tried to force the words out. "It's north of t-town, and people call it th-th-the H-Huh-Hawaii House," said David.

And at that moment, the memory of his first and only visit to that strange place flooded back into Lewis, and he almost leaped up in alarm. For one freezing second the day turned dark, the air grew thick, and from somewhere, from everywhere, Lewis seemed to hear the sound of ominous drums.

CHAPTER 5

Jonathan Barnavelt's 1935 Muggins Simoon was an old-fashioned, long black car with running boards, a squared-off roof, and a horn that gave a deep, throaty "Ah-HOOO-gah!" when you pressed the button. As it rolled through the streets of New Zebedee, people stared at the grand old auto with surprised smiles.

Usually Lewis liked riding in the antique car, but that afternoon he sat huddled in the backseat, dreading their arrival at David's home. It was nearly six o'clock, and after the shock of David's announcing were he lived had more or less passed, Lewis and Rose Rita had spent several hours walking around New Zebedee with David. Just as they were leaving Lewis's house, Uncle Jonathan had called Lewis aside for a quiet word: "It might be better if you didn't say anything about, ah, where David and his family live," he said. "Pass the word to Rose Rita when you have a chance."

Lewis did so, and after that, Rose Rita had talked with a kind of forced cheer, rushing her words and smiling too broadly. Lewis had been too apprehensive and depressed to say anything much, and David seemed to catch his uneasy mood. When Rose Rita would explain something, like how an old abandoned opera house lay above some of the stores downtown, he would nod and give a weak smile, but he wouldn't even try to make a comment or ask a question.

Just after they returned to 100 High Street, Rose Rita had to leave—her dad didn't mind her visiting Lewis, because Uncle Jonathan was pretty well off financially and Rose Rita's dad thought that if people had enough money, they were not weird, only eccentric. On the other hand, Mr. Pottinger considered Mrs. Zimmermann an oddball and didn't like Rose Rita's hanging around her. Mr. Pottinger telephoned just before six, and when Mrs. Zimmermann answered at the Barnavelt home, he told her in a quick, impatient voice that it was time for Rose Rita to return home for dinner. "Better hurry," advised Mrs. Zimmermann. "He sounded a bit gruff."

With Rose Rita gone, Uncle Jonathan, Mrs. Zimmermann, and Lewis were left to take David home. Mrs. Zimmermann had hurried over to her house next door for a shawl, she said, but when she came back, she not only wore a thin purple crocheted shawl over her shoulders, but she also carried a tightly furled umbrella. "Never can tell about these sudden September rainstorms," she remarked brightly. The blue sky was absolutely cloudless and clear, and David looked at Mrs. Zimmermann as if he thought she must be a little crazy.

Uncle Jonathan got his favorite cane out of the tall blue Willoware vase in the front hall, and then he pulled the old Muggins Simoon out of the garage and around to the front of the house, where they all piled in. David kept giving Lewis quizzical looks, but Lewis wasn't in the mood to talk. More than that, he was afraid of what might happen when they took David home to the Hawaii House, because Lewis knew what could happen when Mrs. Zimmermann and his uncle armed themselves with their umbrella and cane.

It took only a few minutes to reach the overgrown lane that led off the highway and into the dark woods. Lewis hadn't been that way in weeks, and to his surprise the lane had been bulldozed flat. Then truckloads of gravel had been dumped on it and spread out into a rough, crunching drive. A red and white sign beside the driveway read:

ANOTHER HAPPY HOME
SOLD!
BY BISHOP BARLOW, REALTOR

Below that was the phone number of Mr. Barlow's realty company. Though the sun was just sinking low and the westward sky still glowed with salmon pink light, the winding driveway seemed drained and dark, and Lewis felt his insides clench tighter and tighter.

The old car rounded the last rumbling curve. It slowed as they approached the Hawaii House, looking just as Lewis remembered it, except that the overgrown shrubs and weeds around it had been hacked completely away and the eroded gully that ran along the front of the house had been filled in. Someone must have planted grass seed, because a thick scattering of hay covered the raw earth all around the place and here and there spears of tender green grass had thrust through the yellow straw. With all the brush cut away, Lewis could see that many stout brick pillars supported the house about five feet off the ground. A crisscross wood lattice painted a deep green made it look as though there were a short lower story, but now Lewis could see light leaking through all the way from the backyard. Probably there was nothing beneath the house but a crawl space, unusual in Michigan because that made the place harder to heat in the winters. In front of the house, Mr. Keller's black Chevrolet was parked

45

close to the steps. Uncle Jonathan pulled up behind it and boomed, "Well, here we are! We'd come in and meet your parents, but—"

"Thuh-th-thanks," began David in a small voice.

"Eh?" said Uncle Jonathan. "You'd like us to meet them? Why, that's very kind of you! Let's go!"

David's face flamed. Lewis knew that Uncle Jonathan was determined to have a look inside the Hawaii House, but the thought of stepping inside the doorway made Lewis feel sick. Everything about the place, from the dark shadows beneath the surrounding trees to the sickly green of the grass struggling up through the hay, made him sense that some great brooding evil had settled here, and that it *wanted* something.

CHAPTER 6

THEY CLIMBED OUT OF the car and David led the way up the veranda steps. At the top, Uncle Jonathan suddenly took a sort of sideways step, blocking David from opening the door. Jonathan held his cane near the brass ferrule on the bottom end and pointed with the globe, making big, sweeping gestures. "Wonderful construction in these fine old houses! Look how neatly the columns meet the roof way up there! Notice how the balcony over us isn't even sagging! Hmmm . . . marvelous, marvelous!"

All the time he ran the globe past and over the wood, staring fixedly at the crystal instead of the things he was pretending to look at. The globe seemed to glow with an icy, winter's-afternoon kind

47

of light, but it always did that. As far as Lewis could see, Uncle Jonathan didn't find anything to alarm him. At last he nodded to Mrs. Zimmermann.

She stepped smartly up to the green front door and rapped on it with her knuckles, three deliberate, slow knocks. They boomed amazingly loud, as though she had pounded on one of those big, cylindrical island drums that Lewis had seen in movies about the South Seas. David looked truly puzzled—he still had his hand stretched out for the doorknob, though Uncle Jonathan had stepped in his way.

A moment later, a woman with dark circles under her eyes and an untidy nest of mousy brown hair opened the door, her mouth drawn into an O of surprise. "David," she said, sounding flustered and pushing a drooping strand of her hair back into place. "Oh, my stars, we lost all track of time—hello, I'm Evelyn Keller," she said to Mrs. Zimmermann.

"How do you do?" Mrs. Zimmermann asked, her voice warm. "My name is Florence Zimmermann, and this is my neighbor Jonathan Barnavelt and his nephew, Lewis. Why, thank you, we'd love to see your amazing new home."

"Uh—yes," said Mrs. Keller, her tired eyes fluttering as if she were having trouble remembering inviting them all in. But she stepped aside and said, "Um, yes, um, come in, please, and please forgive the mess."

"Oh, don't worry about that. We know that moving is always a little messy," said Uncle Jonathan with a broad smile.

Mrs. Zimmermann stepped not inside the house, but onto the threshold, and very softly and quickly she murmured, "Blessings be on this home."

"Wh-what?" asked Mrs. Keller, her voice sounding a lot like her son's.

"Just a little welcoming prayer I learned as a girl," said Mrs. Zimmermann, stepping past her to get inside. "My great-grandmother on my father's side was a very religious woman, one of the Pennsylvania Moravian Extra-Reformed Protestants, you know, and oh, my, isn't this a lovely parlor."

Like a small piece of driftwood caught in a tide, Lewis had been swept into the Hawaii House along with everyone else. "What are they doing?" David whispered to him, without a trace of his stutter.

Lewis managed a weak smile. "Just trying to be friendly," he replied, though he knew that both his uncle and Mrs. Zimmermann were testing the house, trying to detect any strange magic it might hold. Hoping they wouldn't find anything, he stared around at the high-ceilinged room. The walls soared up and up, and he realized that although from the outside the house looked as if it had three floors, in fact it could only have two. This one room was as tall as two regular rooms stacked on top of each other. High up, fancy plaster molding ran around the base of the ceiling, cast into pineapple and palm-tree shapes. The tall windows all along the veranda let the afternoon light stream in.

The other three walls were broken up by a number of very tall, arched built-in shelves, running from the floor almost to the lofty ceiling. Some of these were empty, but some of them were crammed with small objects. Lewis could glimpse wooden ship models, tarnished brass navigating instruments like sextants and dividers and compasses, seashells curiously curved and delicately colored, and a hundred other trinkets and geegaws. A dozen huge cardboard boxes, nearly the size of small trunks, lay scattered about the floor. They had different brand names printed on the sides, like Kellogg's Corn Flakes and Armour Star Canned Hams, and they were all sealed up with brown tape. Lewis supposed they contained dishes and curtains and other stuff that the Kellers had not had time to unpack.

Mrs. Zimmermann walked the edges of the room, clutching her umbrella, her sharp gaze darting this way and that. "My heavens, look at all this fascinating memorabilia. You must be quite a collector!" she said in a strained, though admiring, tone.

"Not really," admitted Mrs. Keller. "Most of this bric-a-brac came with the house. I'm not sure I like it at all. It's like living in a museum! But my husband says there may be some valuable antiques here, so we haven't thrown anything out."

"Hello!" came a new voice, and David's dad came

into the room. His shirt sleeves were rolled up, and streaks of brownish black grease stained his hands and wrists. He clutched a monkey wrench, and what little hair he had frizzed out at the sides.

"Oh," Mrs. Keller said. "This is my husband, Ernest. Ernest, this is Mrs. Zimmermann and, uh—"

"Jonathan Van Olden Barnavelt, at your service!" said Uncle Jonathan. "I would shake your hand, but you've been busy!"

With an embarrassed grin, Mr. Keller said, "Well, yes I have. You see, the water has been cut off for years and years, and I've been under the house trying to get the rusty main valve to turn to the on position. Right now, the only water we have is from an outside tap, and—"

"Say no more!" said Uncle Jonathan. "I am a wizard at unclogging fouled drains, freeing rusty taps, and especially at opening recalcitrant valves! Your good wife was just about to take Mrs. Zimmermann on a quick tour of your home—"

"I was?" asked Mrs. Keller in a weak voice.

Uncle Jonathan did not seem to notice the interruption, but plowed right on:—"and that will give you and me an ample opportunity to bring that valve back to a sense of its proper duty. Lewis, you and David stay here in this room. Touch nothing, do you understand?"

Lewis nodded. David's eyes were big and round,

and when Uncle Jonathan and Mr. Keller left toward the back of the house and Mrs. Keller led Mrs. Zimmermann off to see the hallway and bedrooms, David demanded, "Wh-wh-what are thuh-they u-u-p to?"

Lewis grimaced. He was basically very honest, and he didn't like lying to David, but what could he do? If only Rose Rita had come, she would have no problem spinning out some complicated but believable yarn about why Uncle Jonathan and Mrs. Zimmermann were behaving so strangely, but he felt pretty helpless. "Well," he said slowly, "you have to understand that everybody in New Zebedee is pretty curious about this house. It's been empty for a long time, and I guess they've just been wondering what kind of shape it's in. Mr. Barlow is kind of a sharp operator, people say, and my uncle might want to be sure that he didn't cheat your family when he sold them this place."

David gave Lewis a very suspicious look.

Desperately trying to change the subject, Lewis walked to one of the tall, narrow shelves and picked up a bottle that had inside it a wooden model of a two-masted schooner. The hull was a deep blue, with a yellow stripe running around it, and the fore and aft sails were a sort of creamy tan color, like aged canvas. In tiny little white letters on the bow, the name *Sword* had been written in decorative script. Lewis marveled at how detailed the craft was. He said to David, "This is pretty neat. Do you and your dad build models or something?"

David shook his head. "N-n-no. All, all th-that suh-stuff w-was here when we muh-moved in, like Muh-Mom t-told you. I g-guess the muh-man who b-built the h-house made it."

Lewis put the ship in a bottle down as if it had turned boiling hot. Just as he did, he felt the hair rising on the back of his neck and on his arms. Someone was groaning in terrible pain! It started out as a low sound, like "Ohhhhhhhhhh," and then it became a rising moan, "Mmmmmooooooooo," and it rose even further, into a wild, insane shriek, "Eewweeeee!"

David jumped about a foot and yelped, "What's that?"

If only he could get his frozen legs to work, Lewis was ready to run out of the house, down the drive, and all the way back to his house, but at that moment the unearthly sound died away, and from outside he heard Jonathan's hearty voice: "We've done it! The old pipes are complaining, but now you'll have water!"

A few seconds later, Mr. Keller and Uncle Jonathan tramped in again, and Mr. Keller rushed straight down the hall to the right, the opposite direction from that taken by Mrs. Zimmermann and Mrs. Keller. Lewis heard a gushing, gurgling noise, and then Mr. Keller yelled, "It's rusty-looking and it sounds like a screaming Mimi, but the water's running in the kitchen!"

Uncle Jonathan paused to ask, "Everything all right, Lewis?"

When Lewis nodded, Uncle Jonathan raised his voice: "Excellent, Ernest, since we both need to wash our grimy hands!"

Mrs. Keller and Mrs. Zimmermann returned, with Mrs. Keller asking, "Ernest, what in the world is that horrible noise?"

A beaming Mr. Keller came from the kitchen, wiping his hands on a white towel embroidered with pale blue ducks. "We have water!" he announced. "The taps may look like antiques, but they work. All the rust has cleared up, the water is running clear, and now we can make this place livable. Oh, Mr. Barnavelt, the guest bathroom is the first door on the left. There's some Borax hand soap and some old towels in there if you want to wash up."

"It's Jonathan, and I would love to scrub my hands, thank you very much."

The Kellers, who really seemed to be a very kind couple, shyly invited everyone to stay for dinner—"It's only bologna sandwiches, I'm afraid," said Mrs. Keller apologetically, "but we'd love to share them with you."

Lewis saw Uncle Jonathan dart a quick glance at Mrs. Zimmermann, and he saw her give her head one swift, negative shake. Uncle Jonathan said, "Why, that's very nice of you, Evelyn, but we have things to do. Thank you for letting David come over today, though. We all enjoyed his company, and Lewis and I hope you'll let him visit just as often as he likes."

Mrs. Keller fondly ruffled David's hair. Lewis saw him wince, and from his expression, Lewis understood that David felt embarrassed.

They said their good-byes, and as they approached the old car, Uncle Jonathan asked, "Well, Florence? Did your super-duper magic radar detector find any ghosts or ghouls? Spill everything."

"Shh!" warned Mrs. Zimmermann.

Lewis turned. David stood on the veranda, looking shocked. He must have heard Uncle Jonathan's crack about ghosts.

"Sorry," muttered Jonathan. Once they were in the car, he repeated, "Well? *Did* you detect anything?"

"*You* didn't find anything, I know," returned Mrs. Zimmermann.

"Nothing except a rusty old water valve and a few thousand cobwebs. You know, if the winter is cold, those old pipes under the house are going to freeze and burst, as sure as bunnies come from top hats. I warned Ernest to wrap them all in insulation, though, and maybe he'll take my advice. What could have possessed Abediah Chadwick to build such a ridiculous structure in these parts? But tell me, Florence, *did* you sense anything wrong?"

For a few seconds, Mrs. Zimmermann didn't answer. Then, as if hating to admit it, she said, "No.

Nothing specific. Nobody's cast any evil spells in that house. But there's something I don't like about it, something I can't put my finger on. You must have felt it, too, even though your magical antennae aren't exactly the greatest."

"Well, *I* wouldn't live there," said Jonathan. "I couldn't find anything actively evil either, but you're right about the bad creepy-crawly feeling, like knowing there's a robber hiding quiet beside a lonely road, waiting for you in the dark of night. Lewis, did anything happen when you and David were alone in the living room?"

"No," admitted Lewis. "The racket the pipes made kind of scared us, but that was all."

They didn't say anything else. The car drove on through the evening twilight, turned onto Main Street and then onto Mansion and then High Street, and Jonathan let Mrs. Zimmermann and Lewis out in front of the house before he drove around back to the garage. A few bright stars already glittered overhead. Mrs. Zimmermann put a hand on Lewis's shoulder, lightly. "You're going to have to pay very close attention to your friend David," she said softly. "Think of yourself as a kind of spy. There are dangers around the Keller family, dangers that I cannot even guess at, and you will have to be alert to any hint of them."

Lewis groaned inwardly. He knew he was not brave, and he dreaded the thought of having to check up on

David and having to lie to him. He almost regretted the friendly impulse that had led him to wave David over to the table in the lunchroom at school. But he nodded miserably. "I guess I'll have to do it," he said.

For the next few days, it seemed to Lewis as if he were off the hook. David didn't appear to want his friendship. At school, David tried to eat his lunch as far away from anybody else as he could, slipping to the end of a table where only two or three other kids were sitting. He avoided the bullies as much as possible, and when they caught him, he just balled up his fists, lowered his head, and stubbornly outwaited them. Sometimes he would talk a little to Rose Rita, but he hardly had a word for Lewis.

The next Saturday, while the two of them were sitting in the public library and working on their English homework, Rose Rita tried to explain things to Lewis. "I think Mrs. Zimmermann and your uncle really spooked him. From what little he says, they acted pretty odd when they visited."

"Well," objected Lewis, "they were trying to check out the house to see if nefarious magic spells were at work, like the one old Isaac Izard left behind him in our house."

"But they didn't find anything."

Lewis took a deep breath, inhaling the smells of the library, the ink the librarians used to stamp the date cards, the oily sweeping compound that left the tile floor shiny, and most of all the wonderful, spicy-dusty scent of row on row of books. He hated to admit that his uncle had struck out. "That doesn't mean nothing is wrong," he insisted.

Rose Rita punched her glasses back into place on her nose. "David says he's having bad dreams."

Lewis closed his eyes and thought, I don't want to hear about this.

But Rose Rita went on: "David says that some nights he thinks he hears a lot of drums pounding away in the distance, and other times it's like voices chanting just too far away to be sure he's hearing them at all. And yesterday he said that night before last, he woke up very late, and someone was standing right beside his bed, holding a hand spread out just above his face. David felt like he was frozen. He couldn't move a muscle. He couldn't even breathe."

Lewis wanted to ask her to stop, but he was afraid his voice would squeak out of sheer dread. He shook his head, wanting to signal her to change the subject.

"Then he heard his dad start to snore," continued Rose Rita. "And that made whatever it was fade away. David could breathe again, but he was so scared he couldn't even yell. He hid under his sheet like a little kid until—"

"He told you all that?" asked Lewis.

Rose Rita nodded. "During afternoon study break,"

she said. "Of course, he had a hard time talking about it, but he eventually told me the whole story. He looks awful, Lewis. His eyes are all red and baggy. I don't think he's getting enough sleep."

Lewis said, "Uncle Jonathan made a kind of joke about ghosts. That might explain the dreams." Rose Rita did not reply and at last he asked, "Have you told Mrs. Zimmermann about it?"

"I called her yesterday as soon as I got home from school."

"What did she think?"

Rose Rita shook her head. "She just told me that dreams are dreams, and they can't hurt you. But she said something else. Dreams can be caused by real things. And real things can be pretty dangerous."

They worked on their English assignment for a while longer, but Lewis had a hard time concentrating. He kept imagining what it would be like to wake up in a pitch-dark room, paralyzed. And he kept thinking of how it would be to sense some evil, unseen creature hunched at his bedside and to know that in the darkness an inhuman hand was poised just inches above his face, coming closer and closer, the fingers slightly clenched, the nails like claws....

Lewis shivered. He couldn't help imagining what it must have been like for David, and he wanted more than ever not to have to go any further with the whole business. If something like that horrible dream happened to him, if he had an experience like the one David had described to Rose Rita—

Well, Lewis thought, he would just about lose his mind.

CHAPTER 7

SEPTEMBER WORE ON, AND the maples began to glow yellow and red. The days were still warm, but evenings began to grow chilly, and one morning Lewis woke up to see the delicate lace of frost on his bedroom window. He settled down into the routine of school and grew used to dashing from one class to another one.

David became a little less skittish, and from time to time he would talk to Lewis about this and that—but never about any nightmares. He didn't want to discuss his house either, or his family. Lewis didn't care to bring up the subject of ghosts, so they had little to talk about. Rose Rita was right, though: David looked terrible, as if he never got enough sleep. He had lost some weight, and his bloodshot eyes darted at any sudden sound. Lewis couldn't help feeling sorry for him. Like David, once or twice in his life Lewis had been burdened by troubles and secrets he was reluctant to discuss with anyone, even his uncle. Still, he couldn't force David to open up. All he could do was to give his new friend some time and a sympathetic ear. And there was a lot to like about David: He didn't fight the bullies, but he didn't back down either. He was very smart at math and he liked baseball almost as much as Rose Rita did. Lewis liked him, though he found the friendship a little difficult to maintain when he had to be so careful not to bring up subjects that would upset David.

Late one Friday afternoon toward the end of the month, Uncle Jonathan asked Lewis if David was ever going to come over again. "I don't know," confessed Lewis. "He doesn't seem to get away from home very much."

They were sitting in the parlor of 100 High Street, watching the evening news on the nifty Zenith Stratocaster television set that Uncle Jonathan had installed. It had a gleaming wood cabinet and a perfectly circular screen, like the porthole of a ship. Lewis gazed at the flickering black-and-white image of a weatherman who was explaining that the weekend would be partly cloudy with some chance of rain. Lewis was lying on his side on the sofa, his neck propped up with a plush cushion that had a red maple leaf on it, together with the words "Souvenir of Halifax." Lewis had never been to Halifax and in fact was not quite sure of exactly where it was, but Uncle Jonathan's house was full of odds and ends like that.

Uncle Jonathan sat silent for a long time. He had a pipe in his mouth. Some time back, he had been through a bout of bronchitis and had given up smoking on a dare from Mrs. Zimmermann, who herself had once smoked funny little crooked cigars. He had double-dog-dared her to quit too, and neither of them now touched tobacco, but when he was feeling thoughtful, Jonathan still liked to clench his teeth on a pipe. If he were in a good mood, sometimes he would cast a magic spell so that the bowl glowed bright colors and huge, wonderful shimmering bubbles popped out of the pipe, filled with lifelike figures doing odd things: Mr. Beemuth, the bald, stern-faced science teacher might be seen wearing a kilt and playing the bagpipes, or a little figure that looked like Lewis might be riding a bucking bronco while juggling three lemon meringue pies. Jonathan was not in a particularly frivolous mood that afternoon, so the pipe bowl remained dark and bubbleless.

After a few thoughtful minutes, Jonathan said, "Well, if David was scared by our visit to his house, that's understandable. Florence and I had to get in somehow and check things out, and we may have been too blundering and obvious for his peace of mind. Maybe you could go over to his house some afternoon, just to make sure nothing odd is going on."

Lewis's face felt hot. "I'm no good at that!" he objected. "Rose Rita is braver than I am and smarter than I am, so if you want someone to spy on the Kellers, ask her."

Uncle Jonathan looked startled. He turned in his chair and took the pipe from his mouth, his eyes wide. Then he said, "Oh, Lewis, don't take what I said the wrong way. Sure, I'm worried about the Kellers, and about the Hawaii House. Whatever happened there nearly eighty years ago has the funny taste of the uncanny about it. But I wasn't criticizing you or questioning your courage, and I would never ask you to put yourself into danger."

"I'm not afraid," insisted Lewis.

"Of course not," replied his uncle. "I never thought you were." He sighed. "All right, let's leave it at this: If David asks for your help, or if he begins to talk about anything that sounds odd, let me know. That's not spying—it's just being friendly. If this business is getting to you, I'd rather you stay on the sidelines. All right?"

"All right," muttered Lewis, though he felt as if he had let David down somehow.

Uncle Jonathan stood up and stretched. As usual, he was dressed casually in khaki wash pants, a blue long-sleeved shirt, and his old red vest with four pockets. The vest hung open, but now Uncle Jonathan carefully buttoned it up. "It won't be long before the weather turns cold for keeps," he said. "These balmy evenings aren't long for this world. Let's see if Rose Rita wants to join us on an excursion downtown, and we'll gorge ourselves on banana splits. I'm in a walking mood!"

Lewis loved banana splits. He still felt a little guilty, because his uncle rarely asked anything of him. Uncle Jonathan had a knack of treating Lewis as if he were an adult, and somehow he had enough kid in him to meet Lewis more than halfway. Now when Uncle Jonathan made a simple request, Lewis couldn't get up the nerve to do as he asked. Something about the Hawaii House scared him, and he never wanted to go there again.

Uncle Jonathan paused in the front hall to take his favorite cane from the blue vase, and as he did, he happened to glance into the little round mirror on the coat rack. He had idly enchanted the mirror many years before, so that sometimes instead of reflecting your face it showed random scenes from exotic corners of the world, and sometimes it received radio broadcasts from WGN in Chicago. Every so often it also dipped into history or what seemed to be the future, and it had given Lewis glimpses of a team of workers building an Egyptian pyramid and a giant rocket blasting off into the heavens. Jonathan took a step back and lowered his chin as he stared into the mirror, muttering, "Hum! That's strange. I've never seen anything quite like that before."

Lewis craned around him and saw that the circle of glass pulsated and flickered with brilliant flashes of orange light. An incandescent fountain jetted up, turned ruddy, and then fell in glowing globs through the dark air again. It looked very much like the fountain downtown, if the fountain had been made of glaring light instead of water. "What is it?"

Uncle Jonathan shook his head. "I'm not sure. This doesn't have the feel of something from the past or future, and I don't think it's just an imaginary scene. If I had to guess, I'd say we are seeing the eruption of a shield volcano, like the ones that blew their stacks in Iceland not long ago. They're the ones that produce fountains of lava instead of the huge black clouds of ash that a conical volcano produces. But the news broadcast didn't say a word about a volcanic eruption anywhere on earth."

Lewis asked apprehensively, "Could that be a warning that one is going to erupt around here?"

"Hardly," replied Uncle Jonathan. "The geology of Michigan doesn't support any kind of volcano that I know of. That kind of volcano is more common in—" Jonathan broke off suddenly, his expression troubled. But then he shrugged. "Oh, well, this doojigger doesn't always show just what's really happening. Every once in a while it decides to give us a scene of green and red macaws in top hats dancing in a chorus line or a football game where one side wears pink ballet tutus and the other is dressed in tuxedos and skin-diving masks."

Uncle Jonathan didn't appear to be perturbed, and Lewis didn't think anything more about the mirror. Lewis telephoned Rose Rita, and she agreed at once to join them. Then he and his uncle walked toward town though a cool, pleasant twilight. As they strolled down Mansion Street, Rose Rita popped out of her house and hurried to join them. "Hello!" Uncle Jonathan said cheerfully. "Greetings, salutations, and welcome aboard. Now, before I get myself in trouble with your folks for spoiling your appetite, have you had dinner?"

"Just finished it," said Rose Rita. "Pork chops and sauerkraut, which I don't particularly like."

"No dessert? Good," returned Uncle Jonathan. "Then if you still have room, you can sneak off with us and savor some frozen delights. I seem to remember you have a fondness for strawberry sundaes, and the calories are on me tonight."

"Where's Mrs. Zimmermann?" asked Rose Rita as she fell into step beside them.

"She is busy with a research project," Uncle Jonathan said shortly. Lewis wondered about that, because as far as he knew, they hadn't heard anything from Mrs. Zimmermann that afternoon. As if he wanted to change the subject, Uncle Jonathan asked, "How is school, Rose Rita?"

Beside Lewis, Rose Rita made a grunt of dissatisfaction. "Not great," she said. "I keep telling everyone that I don't like home economics, and they keep telling me that someday I'll get *married* and want to be a *homemaker*."

"There's nothing wrong with being either of those things," observed Uncle Jonathan.

Lewis sensed rather than saw Rose Rita's shrug. "Maybe not, but I want to be a famous writer. I want to be so rich that I can hire someone else to do all the cooking and cleaning for me while I travel the world and write stories and have autograph parties."

Uncle Jonathan laughed. "Good for you! Be exactly what you want, and don't mind what anyone else says, that's my motto."

The streetlights had just flickered on when the three of them reached Main Street. Everything was still and peaceful as could be, with almost no traffic and only a few people out on the sidewalks. They turned toward the soda fountain and at that instant, Lewis heard a screech of brakes and spun to take a panicky look at what was barreling down the street behind him.

CHAPTER 8

CLATTERING AND LURCHING TOWARD them with two screeching wheels on the sidewalk and blue smoke spitting from under its tortured tires was the town garbage truck. It was speeding right for them, mowing down parking meters as if they were stalks of wheat, approaching too fast, already too close to avoid—

Umph! Something hit Lewis right in the stomach, and he tumbled down, heels over head. In the next heartbeat the runaway truck screamed past, so close that a blast of wind from it whipped Lewis's hair and the dust it kicked up stung the skin on his neck and the back of his hands. The top of a decapitated parking meter crashed through a window behind him, and a shower of glass fell close to him, making him throw his arms around his head.

For a moment, Lewis thought the truck had run over him, and he waited frantically to feel the pain of broken bones and gashed flesh. Gradually he realized that, aside from scratched knees, he was safe and whole. Everything seemed to go in slow motion, though mere seconds had passed.

From somewhere came the shattering sound of a crash and a crunch, then the clatter of flying metal and the tinkle of glass. Someone was screaming like a maniac. Lewis felt hands helping him up, and he heard Uncle Jonathan's shaky, anxious voice: "Are you both all right?"

That was when Lewis realized that Uncle Jonathan had reacted with the reflexes of a football guard. He had shoved Rose Rita and Lewis down, rolling them over onto the narrow strip of grass in front of Corrigan's hardware store a moment before leaping back, barely avoiding the runaway truck the way a matador would spin away from an enraged bull. The garbage truck must have whizzed right between them, missing them all by a matter of a few inches.

"I'm not hurt," gasped Rose Rita. "Lewis?"

"Okay," was all Lewis could say, as he wondered if whoever was yelling might be pinned under the tires of the truck. "Uncle Jonathan, did it hit you?"

Grimly, Uncle Jonathan said, "It missed me by about one-tenth the thickness of a baby gnat's eyebrow. That Potsworth Stevenson must have been drinking on the job. Look what he's done!"

Down the street, not far past the drugstore, the garbage truck had plowed into the rear of a parked Ford, forcing the car forward right into a telephone pole, which had splintered and now stood partly bent over the two wrecked vehicles. The truck had snapped off about ten parking meters, and they lay scattered like jackstraws on the sidewalk. Broken fragments of glass gleamed in the streetlights, and from under the crumpled hood of the garbage truck thick white steam jetted out with a hiss that sounded like a giant snake. The odd sweet smell of antifreeze filled the air. People were gathering around the truck, and from inside the cab the driver was trying to force the door open, but the metal had bent and buckled. The screams were pouring from the garbage truck's partially opened window, high and shrill.

A man had climbed up onto the running board of the truck and was bellowing through the gap at the top of the window: "Hold on! We called the police. They'll be here in a minute. Just—"

Crash! Smash! The garbage truck driver was swinging something at the windshield from the inside. The man jumped off the running board and ducked away from the danger. More glass flew, and then a frenzied Skunky Stevenson came wriggling and crawling out of the broken windshield like a maggot writhing out of a rotten apple. Lewis saw that in his scratched and bloody hands he held a short crowbar, and he brandished it at the three or four people who had run out to help him. "Stay back!" he wailed. "Get away! Keep them off me!"

"Potsworth!" yelled Uncle Jonathan. "Calm down!" He said quickly to Rose Rita and Lewis, "You two stay here. I think something's wrong with him." He strode forward.

"Help me!" bawled Stevenson. "Here they come! They want to drag me away!" He took a desperate roundhouse swing with the crowbar, like the ball-player Joe DiMaggio taking a hard cut at a fastball, and people jumped away from him, shouting in anger and confusion. Stevenson pointed with the crowbar, past Rose Rita and Lewis. "Oh, saints help me, here they come!" Lewis fearfully looked back, but saw only the deserted, quiet street. Nothing moved there, not even a cat or a dog.

"Potsworth!" Uncle Jonathan had stopped a few steps away from the wreck. He stood right in the center of the street, leaning on his cane, and the other people sort of spread out in a semicircle to either side of him, as if they hoped he could talk some sense into this wild man. "Calm down, old friend. Are you hurt?"

Stevenson collapsed to his knees. The crowbar dropped from his bloody hands and clanged clatter-ing onto the pavement. "Jonny?" he asked in a voice racked by deep, shuddering sobs. "Jonny Barnavelt? Is that you?"

Lewis felt his flesh crawl. Skunky Stevenson's voice had become that of a six-year-old, high and bleating, full of terror. From beside him, Lewis heard Rose Rita gasp at the sound.

Uncle Jonathan took a few steps forward. "It's all right, Pots," he said in a gentle voice. "I can see that you've scratched yourself up pretty badly, but we'll send for Doc Humphries and—"

"Keep them away!" shouted Stevenson, suddenly leaping up and throwing his hands in front of him, as if he were fending off some invisible attacker. "Oh, Mother of Mercy, don't let them get me!"

In the corner of Lewis's eye something moved, across the street, some fleeting and stealthy gray shape, or many gray shapes hurrying past in a single line. He whirled to look—and nothing was there except for the five-and-dime and the feed and seed company. He remembered the very first time he and Rose Rita had seen the Hawaii House, how he'd had the eerie sensation that a row of ghostly marchers scurried beside them as they retreated back toward the highway. This was just like that—

"Here!" Stevenson had taken something from his pocket. "It was in their garbage, they didn't want it! Oh, take it, take it, it's yours and you can have it, but leave me my soul!" With a convulsive jerk of his arm, he threw something small, something invisible at that distance. Except that when it arched high in the dusk, it caught fire, first as a little red glowing ember about the size of a marble. Then it flared to white-hot life, streaked down toward the earth trailing flames behind it, and landed with a splat in the street off to Lewis's left. Where it hit, it burst into a sparkling spatter of liquid, fiery drops, just like—

Just like the molten lava pictured in the enchanted mirror.

Lewis felt chilled. Uncle Jonathan had been about to say that volcanoes like the one in the mirror were more common in places like—Hawaii!

"What just happened?" asked Rose Rita in an unsteady voice. "Lewis, did you feel that?"

"Yeah." Something had gone away. Lewis could feel it pass, the way a sudden breeze could spring up and then die away. The whole world seemed to let out a long-held breath.

Ahead of them, Skunky Stevenson slowly collapsed to the dark asphalt beside his wrecked truck, whimpering like a little baby, then making a horrible keening sound, rising and rising in pitch until Lewis wanted to clap his hands over his ears to shut it out.

More and more people showed up, coming out of the few stores that were still open, but nobody ventured close to the fallen man. From down toward the fountain a siren howled, and Lewis could see the flashing red light of a police car tear through the roundabout. It screeched to a halt, and two policemen climbed out, staring at the wreck and at the crowd. Maybe a dozen people stood around Stevenson in a silent circle, but not a single one moved to help him until Uncle Jonathan stepped forward. One of the policemen cautioned, "Better watch out, Mr. Barnavelt. He may be dangerous."

"He isn't," replied Uncle Jonathan firmly. He knelt beside the weeping man, one knee in the puddle of water that had leaked from the truck radiator, and patted the huddled, weeping figure on the shoulder. "It's all right," Uncle Jonathan said over and over. "Nobody's going to hurt you now. They've gone away, Potsworth. It's all right."

But it wasn't. Lewis felt sick and dizzy from the close call and from the way the fallen man could not stop crying. The sobbing, gibbering noises were horrible. They were the sounds of someone who had completely lost his mind.

CHAPTER 9

I T WAS NINE O'CLOCK. Rose Rita, Uncle
Jonathan, and Lewis had not enjoyed any
ice-cream treats, but had instead gone to Mrs. Zimmermann's house, where they had a council of war
in her living room. She had turned on every lamp
and light, and the purple furnishings nearly glowed.
Over the mantel a purple dragon writhed in a framed
painting. Lewis found it hard even to look at the creature, so he kept his eyes on the toes of his sneakers.

Mrs. Zimmermann was pacing the floor while the
other three sat on her overstuffed purple sofa. "It
was a pearl?" she asked Uncle Jonathan. "Are you
sure?"

"I'm not sure about anything," confessed Uncle
Jonathan. "And especially not about what Potsworth

Stevenson thought he was taking from the Kellers' trash. He told me he found a wooden box in the Kellers' garbage can, about yay by yay"—here Uncle Jonathan indicated a square about four inches on a side—"and he thought he might be able to sell it. He found a secret compartment in the blasted thing, and inside that was what he thought to be a pearl the size of a robin's egg."

"A pearl?" Rose Rita asked.

"Hawaii was once famous for its pearls," returned Uncle Jonathan. "That's how Pearl Harbor got its name. I have no doubt that old Captain Chadwick brought back a few."

Mrs. Zimmermann stopped pacing, folded her arms across her chest, and shook her head. "Pearls. This is nothing I've heard of. I know of earth magic and water magic and sky magic—even of weather magic, like the kind the late, unlamented Isaac Izard used to practice. But *pearl* magic? Never. What happened to it?"

"He threw it away," said Rose Rita. "And it burned up in the air."

Mrs. Zimmermann gave her an astonished look. "Wha-a-at?"

"I saw it too. It looked like molten lava," added Lewis in a small voice. "It hit the street and then just boiled away to nothing."

"Just a sooty mark like a black asterisk," agreed Uncle Jonathan. "Remember when we were kids and we used to set off fireworks and sometimes they'd leave a burned patch? It was like that."

Mrs. Zimmermann sniffed. "Some of us never fooled around with dangerous things like firecrackers. Well, this beats everything I've ever run across. Is Potsworth all right?"

Uncle Jonathan coughed. "Well, no. I don't think he'll ever be all right again. The doctors don't think he's physically injured—at least they couldn't find any broken bones, though he's got some bad lacerations on his hands from breaking out the windshield of his truck—but he's having terrible hallucinations. He told me that an army was after him, an army of ghosts made of night and darkness."

"I felt them," said Lewis. He told about his two experiences, first at the Hawaii House and then on Main Street. "I couldn't see anything when I looked straight at them," he finished. "But when I was looking away, they sort of flickered off to one side. It was like a whole bunch of people darting along, in single file."

Mrs. Zimmermann frowned. "Did you get any impression of them? How big were they? Human-sized? Bigger? Smaller?"

Lewis felt helpless. "I don't really know. Human-sized, I think. Taller than me."

Turning to Rose Rita, Mrs. Zimmermann asked, "And did you see or sense anything?"

"No!" Rose Rita said, sounding bewildered. "And

Lewis never mentioned seeing anything before either."

Lewis hung his head. "I didn't want to sound like a scaredy-cat," he mumbled. "And I don't want to lose my mind like Sku—Mr. Stevenson."

Mrs. Zimmermann's mouth set itself into a grim, straight line. "I don't like this. I don't like this at all. Lewis, since you've seen these figures, they may have their eyes on you too. You're going to have to be brave. Something bad is going on, something ancient and deep and beyond my knowledge. I was worried about David and his family." She looked into Lewis's eyes. "But now," she added sorrowfully, "now I'm most worried about you."

CHAPTER 10

SKUNKY STEVENSON'S ACCIDENT WAS less than a nine days' wonder. At the first of the week, he was sent away to a special hospital in Westland, a town some distance east of New Zebedee. A couple of hulking, beeping wreckers had long since towed the dented old garbage truck and the ruined Ford away. The telephone company had even replaced the splintered pole. People talked about what had happened, to be sure, but by Tuesday, almost everything was back to normal, although if you knew just where to look in the center of Main Street, you could still see the inky splat where the flaming pearl, if it was a pearl, had landed. That spot seemed to be seared right down into the surface, like a brand burned into cowhide.

Lewis couldn't stand not knowing whether David had seen the same ghostly figures as he had. So at lunch on the last Wednesday in September, Lewis made a determined effort to talk to David. He finally glimpsed the boy actually sitting outside the lunchroom. David had slipped out a side door—you weren't supposed to do that, of course—and sat crouched in a hard-to-see spot at the corner of the school, huddled miserably with his back against the brick wall, his lunch tray balanced across his knees. Lewis took a look around to make sure no one was noticing him, and then he ducked outside too. "Hi," he said.

David didn't say a word, but stared down at his ketchup-coated meat loaf, shriveled green peas, congealed carrots, and hard-as-a-rock peanut butter cookie. Lewis hunkered down beside him and with a shock noticed that David had a split lip with a short wound that looked ugly and reddish brown, and a swollen purplish bruise beside his left eye. "What happened?" asked Lewis, so concerned that he decided against asking David about the ghostly figures.

Raising a hand to hide his face, David mumbled, "N-nothin'. R-ruh-ran into a duh-door."

"Nuts," said Lewis, anger rising in him against whoever had done this. "Somebody beat you up, didn't they?"

"I duh-don't w-want t-to t-talk ab-buh-about it,"

81

insisted David, his face flushing. His voice sounded as if it were about to break into sobs.

Lewis crossed his arms. The weather had turned cooler, and he wasn't wearing a jacket. He could see goose pimples on David's neck. David picked at the meal with no real sign of an appetite. With a sigh, Lewis said, "Listen, who hit you?" A sick thought suddenly rose in his mind, and he lowered his voice: "It wasn't your dad, was it?"

"No!" David's sharp answer came right away. His lips tightened, and his eyes filled with tears. "My dad hasn't ever hit me," he said with no trace of a stutter. Then he bit his swollen lip and dropped his gaze down to the ground. Quietly, he admitted, "It was th-that Muh-M-Mike D-Dugan, a-after suh-school y-yesterday."

"You should have told—"

David was shaking his head. "H-he suh-said w-we'd k-killed S-Skunky S-Stevenson."

"What?" Lewis asked, his voice an outraged squawk.

"Everybody knew th-that h-he c-came from our p-place just before the wreck. The p-police t-told s-some people that M-Mr. S-Stevenson was s-say-ing we h-hexed him somehow, we t-trapped him by throwing away that b-box—"

"That's crazy," said Lewis furiously. "And anyway, Skunky Stevenson isn't even dead. He's in a mental hospital in another town. And you didn't cause it to happen. He stole something, and it drove him out of his mind. Anyway, he's been sort of off the tracks for years and years. Mike didn't have any right to hit you. Look, you ought to tell a teacher or—"

David shook his head. "No. I w-won't. D-don't you either. Puh-promise me, L-Lewis."

Lewis got a little inkling of the frustration that Uncle Jonathan must have felt kneeling beside the fallen Mr. Stevenson that night when no one else would step forward and Mr. Stevenson couldn't stop wailing. "You should," he insisted.

David gave him a pleading look. "I d-don't want to c-cause trouble."

Lewis didn't answer right away. "Look," he said at last, "Rose Rita and I really like you. If anybody else picks on you or even looks at you funny, you tell me or Rose Rita, okay?"

David pressed his lips into a straight line and gave a weak nod. His expression was troubled, but he didn't want to talk, and Lewis couldn't force him. At least, though, Lewis could find them a way back into the lunchroom where no one would pay them much attention. They had to sneak around the corner and into a hall door, but they managed it without bringing down the wrath of a teacher. Lewis had not even had time to eat, but he didn't much feel like tackling the lunchroom food. His stomach churned and he still had that sick feeling whenever he thought about big Mike Dugan whaling away on David. Not that Lewis would have the nerve to tell off Mike. If he tried, he knew he would wind up with bruises and aches, just like David.

That afternoon in science class, Lewis noticed how truly haggard David was looking. They were doing a chemistry lesson. The kids changed lab partners pretty much any way they wanted, and that day Lewis paired up with David, who usually was the odd student working alone at the last table.

The bruises that David had tried to keep hidden showed up clearly in the harsh daylight that streamed through the tall school windows. His left eyelid had a nasty twitch, and his swollen lip looked painful.

Today they were using litmus paper to test various liquids and sorting them as acids or bases. Everyone had ten little test tubes of solutions, some clear as water, others weak transparent colors, green, pale blue, and even a shade of purple that Lewis thought Mrs. Zimmermann would like. The test tubes were labeled A through J. Everyone had to write down the letters of the solutions on a lab-report form. Then they had to use two kinds of litmus paper, blue and pink. A blue strip turned pink in acid, and a pink one turned blue in a base. If neither changed, the liquid was neutral.

It was pretty simple, and Lewis spent more time looking at David's injured face than at the slips of litmus paper. David was trying to concentrate, but twice he made mistakes with the elementary experiment, once writing down that an acid solution was a base, once that a clear neutral solution that Lewis suspected to be plain old tap water was an acid.

Lewis corrected him both times, and when they turned in their answer sheet, he was pretty sure they had scored a hundred. Mr. Beemuth, who was so bald that his head looked sanded and polished, glanced at the paper and nodded. "Good work, boys. You have an accident, Keller?" he asked in an uninterested voice.

David's face turned all red and he nodded miserably.

"Well, be more careful. These are all correct." He put a check mark on the lab sheet and wrote two grades down in his grade book, and that was that.

Lewis nudged David. "All right, partner," he said, trying to sound cheerful. "We aced that one, didn't we?"

At that moment, someone dropped a test tube, and it shattered on the floor. It was no big deal.

Except that David flinched so hard at the sound that he looked as if he'd just been shot. Lewis felt a surge of sympathy. He knew what that kind of fear was like. And he wished he could somehow make it go away.

But how? That was the question he couldn't answer: How?

CHAPTER 11

THERE WAS ONLY ONE way, and that was to gain David's trust again. As soon as school was over, Lewis found David, waiting to board the bus. "Hey," he said, "I meant to ask you, how's the house fixing-up coming along?"

"Okay, I g-guess," said David. "D-Dad s-says he s-still needs to take care of those p-pipes so they d-don't freeze."

"Maybe we can come out and help," suggested Lewis.

"M-maybe," David said as he climbed onto the bus steps.

Lewis grimaced as the yellow bus clattered away. Like most of the town kids, he walked to and from school, and he joined up with Rose Rita as they made their way home. He told her about David, and as he expected, she glowered at the news.

"Mike Dugan is nothing but a bully," she said. "He should be—"

"I know, I know," replied Lewis wearily. "But who's going to tell him off? He'd wipe the floor with me. And you'd embarrass David if you took up for him—everyone would say he was hiding behind a girl."

Rose Rita's eyes flashed, but she reluctantly nodded. "Okay. So how are you going to help him?"

"I can't beat up the bullies, but maybe if David isn't scared of ghosts, he could stand up for himself. I'm going to try to get Uncle Jonathan out there again." Lewis kicked a fallen acorn, sending it spinning into the gutter. "I don't even know why I'm trying to help David," he confessed.

"I do," Rose Rita said. "It's because you don't like to see anybody picked on. And because you know what it's like."

Lewis nodded and thought, It's also because I hate being such a scaredy-cat myself.

When Lewis got home and spoke to Uncle Jonathan, he nodded gravely. "The Kellers really moved into New Zebedee on a shoestring," he said thoughtfully. "Those pipes are something that really shouldn't wait, or they'll find themselves with a sky-high plumbing bill when the pipes freeze and shatter. I have a teeny little suspicion, though, that Ernest may not be able to afford the insulation just yet. Let me see what I can do."

He made a couple of telephone calls, and he wound up by calling the Kellers. They had a party line, which meant they shared their telephone line with two other families. It took Uncle Jonathan a couple of tries to get through. When he finally did, Lewis heard him say, "Hello, Ernest? Jonathan Barnavelt here. . . . Very well, thank you. Listen, have you bought the insulation for your pipes yet? . . . No? Well, then I have some good news. You know, I just remembered that a few years ago I did a little insulating around this old place, and I looked down in the cellar a few minutes ago and saw that I have two full rolls of the stuff left. I don't have any use at all for them, and if you want them, they're yours for free. . . . No, no, I wouldn't charge you a penny. They're just taking up space in my cellar, and I'll be glad to get rid of them. . . . Sure, I can bring them over this weekend, say Saturday morning. I'll come dressed to work, and we'll get everything shipshape in no time. Oh, is it all right if Lewis tags along to visit David? . . . Great, great. . . . You're very welcome."

He hung up the phone and drummed his fingers. "Okay, let's run over to that little hardware store in Crow Corners. Old Pete should have a few rolls of insulation I could buy without paying my eyeteeth. I'd get the stuff at Corrigan's in town, but you know how people like to gossip about nothing. If I bought the insulation here, Mr. Keller would find out soon enough that I fibbed about having some left over, and that would hurt his pride. I don't want him to think that I'm giving him charity. Some people are very sensitive about that."

"Couldn't you just lend him the insulation and let him pay you back later?"

"I could," agreed Uncle Jonathan, "but I won't, for three reasons. First, it's pretty inexpensive, and I can afford it with no trouble or fuss. Second, it's just something I want to do to be neighborly. Most important, though, I'm curious about that house. I want to get out there again and make sure that Florence and I didn't miss anything, and two rolls of insulation is a cheap price to pay for admission!"

The next afternoon they got into the Muggins Simoon and took off in a pale blue cloud of exhaust smoke for Crow Corners, a farming village off on the Homer Road. It was barely a crossroads, with a filling station, general store, and grocery in one small building and a combination hardware and feed store diagonally across from that. Lewis had been in the place before, because old Pete, the toothless, grumbling man who owned it, stocked all sorts of old-fashioned, hard-to-get items that Uncle Jonathan occasionally needed or just wanted. If you wanted a buggy whip or a screech-owl call or a hand-cranked apple corer, you went to Pete's, which was a tightly crammed, dark store that smelled of oily metal, seed corn, and kerosene.

Sure enough, old Pete sold Uncle Jonathan two dusty rolls of insulation that had been stored on a ramshackle shelf in the back of the store so long that Uncle Jonathan's story of having shoved them down cellar and forgotten about them was plausible. Uncle Jonathan heaved both rolls into the trunk and they blatted back to town.

It was a dark, overcast day, and when they got home, Lewis went to the front hall to hang up his coat. The mirror on the coatrack at first looked very ordinary, but then a flash caught Lewis's eye. He felt the hair on the back of his neck standing up. He told himself that an image in a mirror couldn't hurt him and forced himself to look.

He didn't understand what he was seeing at first. It might have been a shield, black against a kind of reddish orange glow. Then the glow brightened, and with a gasp, Lewis realized he was looking at a woman's face, exotic and strange, with a straight nose, a cruel mouth, and closed eyes.

Slowly the eyes opened.

They had no whites or pupils. They were red-hot coals, and flames licked out of the corners, curling away as they rose. The mouth opened, and more fire poured out.

Lewis yelled hoarsely, and in a moment, Uncle Jonathan was at his side. "What happened?"

Lewis pointed a shaking finger, but now the mirror was just a mirror again, and he was only pointing at his own terrified reflection.

When he could talk, he blurted out what he had seen, stammering nearly as much as David. "Did you recognize the face?" asked his uncle.

Lewis shook his head. "She said something, though. I couldn't hear it, but I could sort of read her lips."

"What did she say?" asked Jonathan.

Lewis swallowed at a lump that wouldn't go away. "I think she said, 'Death.'"

Friday evening Rose Rita and Mrs. Zimmermann came over for dinner. Mrs. Zimmermann baked a chicken and served it up with mixed vegetables and boiled potatoes, and as they ate, she grudgingly gave an account of her researches. "I've called, written, or wired every expert I know," she said. "None of them can offer the least bit of help."

Rose Rita's lips pursed in disappointment. Lewis knew that she considered Mrs. Zimmermann her best grown-up friend, and she was always very protective of Mrs. Zimmermann's reputation as a great sorceress. "You'll find it," she said in an encouraging way.

Mrs. Zimmermann smiled but waved off Rose Rita's compliment. "Thank you, but someone with a doctorate in magical arts shouldn't step up to the plate and let three fastballs zip by without even taking a swing, the way I have."

"Don't you have some idea of what's going on?" asked Lewis.

With a wry shrug, Mrs. Zimmermann explained, "Well, I thought at first we might be facing a haunting. Ghostly apparitions can be very strange and sometimes very threatening, but since they aren't magic, or at least not human-type magic, their presence is difficult to detect. However, all my so-called experts gave me some suggestions about how to test that theory, and none of the things they said to look out for have appeared in this case."

"If it isn't magic and it isn't ghosts, what could it be?" asked Rose Rita.

Mrs. Zimmermann gave her a weary smile. "There you have put your finger firmly on the question." She thoughtfully tapped her chin. "Well-l, let me see. It might be a manifestation of elemental spirits. Do you know what those are?"

Lewis shook his head, feeling his chest tighten. Uncle Jonathan stirred, but thought better of answering. Sometimes he confessed to being a little shy when discussing magic with Mrs. Zimmermann, because she had studied the subject at a prestigious foreign university, while he himself simply had a bachelor's degree in agriculture.

Mrs. Zimmermann was ready to answer her own question, and she ticked off the possibilities on her fingers. "Some people, like the Rosicrucians, believe that the world is largely governed by spirits that aren't really ghosts, because they've never had a body. These spirits can control earth, air, fire, and water."

Uncle Jonathan reached for a drumstick. "The old Greeks thought those were the four elements," he explained, gesturing with the chicken leg. "That everything was made up of those four things, in different combinations. So the spirits that inhabit and control them are called elementals."

"But I have never seen an elemental, and neither has your uncle, Lewis," put in Mrs. Zimmermann. "The fact that the pearl, or whatever the thing was, burst into flame made me think that a fire elemental might have stuck his ectoplasmic finger in this pie. But I've read up on that, and nothing else suggests any such thing. Dead end."

"Then there's the idea of a Polynesian demon," added Uncle Jonathan. "That's a kind of spirit too. I've read up on them a little, at Florence's suggestion. She thought about that after I described the woman's face Lewis glimpsed in the hall mirror. There's an old Hawaiian story about a man who offended the island gods, and they punished him by cremating him in red-hot lava. His body all burned away, leaving only his head, which burst into flame and went bobbing and floating along in the air. This fiery head then haunted the area where the man had lived, flying through the night and attacking the villagers. Finally, a wise man lured the head to chase him into a cave, where he'd created a trap of sharpened spears, and the head flew in so fast that it impaled itself—"

"Stop!" pleaded Lewis, dropping his fork. Rose Rita was looking a little green around the gills too.

"It's only an old story," said Uncle Jonathan. "But that didn't pan out, either. There are no volcanoes around here, and Makalani certainly didn't turn into a fiery ghost. She died peacefully in bed."

"Makalani?" asked Rose Rita.

Mrs. Zimmermann was sipping from a cup of coffee. She nodded over the rim. "That's right, we haven't told you, have we? Princess Makalani was the name of Captain Abediah Chadwick's island bride, and don't think it was easy to dig that fact up from the old records."

"Even the local newspapers," put in Uncle Jonathan. "Florence finally found the tale in a university library. A graduate student wrote a master's thesis on local folklore back in 1926 that mentions the Hawaii House."

"Even that was fifty years after the event," took up Mrs. Zimmermann. "Anyway, Chadwick was a secretive man, and no one in New Zebedee got to know his wife at all, except for the servants they kept. On the fateful night of January 19, 1876, the princess simply passed away as if she had gone to sleep and never woke up again. They found her lying

94

in her bed, her black hair spread out over the pillow, with a little smile on her face and her hands crossed peacefully on her breast. Except for one person, everyone else in the house had died the same way, quietly in bed."

"The one person was Abediah Chadwick," said Rose Rita. "You said he froze."

Lewis writhed, imagining how horrible it would be to feel the blood freezing in his veins.

Mrs. Zimmermann appeared almost as uncomfortable as he felt. "Yes, Abediah did die from the cold. In fact, people suspected foul play. Chadwick had fled up to that platform over the veranda and had barricaded himself outside. The temperature was about ten below that night, and they found him in his nightclothes, frozen solid, kneeling and leaning against the stuff he had piled against the door, as if he were trying to keep someone from bursting through."

Uncle Jonathan grunted. "I wish we knew someone who had first-hand experience of Hawaii. I don't even know anyone in town who's ever vacationed there!"

"We're sure not having any luck with books," said Lewis. "I even looked up all the *National Geographic* articles about Hawaii, but they didn't help."

Mrs. Zimmermann nodded slowly. "Well, let's keep trying. Maybe we can think of someone to ask. Meanwhile, let's have Jonathan go ahead with his visit to help save those rusty old pipes from Jack Frost. If we can get along without involving more people, I think we ought to."

Uncle Jonathan nodded his agreement. "I'd hate to put anyone else in town in danger. Let's wait until I've been out to the house again before we begin pulling anyone else we know into this puzzle."

Later, as Lewis walked Rose Rita back home, she suddenly said, "I think my grampa visited Hawaii when he was in the navy. We could ask him!"

Lewis stared at her. "My gosh, Rose Rita, you heard what Mrs. Zimmermann and Uncle Jonathan said! You don't want to put your grampa Galway in danger, do you?"

"No," returned Rose Rita. "But he's seen a thing or three, and he's full of stories about odd places and events. Tell you what: If nothing breaks in the next few days, you and I will go over and talk with him. We won't tell him the whole story, but we can see if he knows anything that might help us."

Lewis could think of no good objection to that, so he muttered a halfhearted agreement. And there matters rested for a couple of days. Lewis kept thinking that somehow things might right themselves, but no such luck. At night he had flashes of bad dreams, feeling his face freezing hard as stone and his eyes staring blindly. And at times he had nightmares of a savage-looking warrior, spear in hand, about to thrust into his chest and—what? Steal his soul?

At any rate, nothing changed. David remained as miserable as ever, and so bright and early on Saturday morning, Uncle Jonathan and Lewis drove over to the Hawaii House to deliver the insulation. The Kellers had finished unpacking, but Lewis saw that they had not moved any of the ship models and other bric-a-brac from the tall living room shelves.

The room gave Lewis the creeps, and he suggested that he and David go outside and toss a football around. Lewis wasn't any good at even so simple a game, but he would rather face a whole football field of tackles than stay inside the Hawaii House.

They didn't talk very much. David listlessly threw the ball in long, lazy loops that should have been easy for anyone to catch. More often than not, though, the ball slipped through Lewis's fingers and bounced crazily off the ground.

Lewis wasn't much better at throwing the ball. He had never gained the knack of putting just the right spin on it, so his passes were wobbly, short, and inaccurate. They were playing in the backyard, which was still covered mostly with hay and with a sparse growth of grass sticking out here and there, like a few hairs combed hopefully across a bald man's head. They could hear Uncle Jonathan and David's dad creeping around under the house, tacking the insulation to the floor joists and ripping off big lengths of tape to bind it around standing pipes and drains.

At last the two men came edging out of the low door in the lattice that surrounded the crawl space, and Uncle Jonathan put both hands in the small of his back as he arched his spine. "Oh, it feels good to stand up without conking my noggin," he said. "Well, Ernest, we had just enough to cover everything. Now you're all set, unless we have a week of thirty-below temperatures, and we don't get very many of those."

Lewis was ready to go right then, but Mr. Keller insisted that everyone had to have lunch. Mrs. Keller had cooked a big pot of spaghetti with meatballs. It tasted wonderful, but Lewis was getting that old flip-floppy feeling in his stomach again.

"Maybe this will keep the pipes from rattling and banging at night," Mrs. Keller said with a wan smile. Like her son, she had dark smudges under her eyes, as if she were not sleeping well.

"Sounds like a Western movie late every evening," Mr. Keller agreed, serving himself another few meatballs. "I'm hoping that by the end of next month I can get the upstairs bedrooms in shape and we can all move in there. Maybe that will put us far enough away so the rattling doesn't bother us."

Jonathan munched a meatball and then asked, "What do you mean, it sounds like a Western movie?"

"Like drums," replied Mr. Keller. "Doesn't it, Evelyn?"

His wife shivered and nodded. "Just like the drums of Apaches, or maybe of South Sea islanders."

Lewis had a mouthful of spaghetti that he couldn't force down. His heart seemed to have scrambled up into his throat.

"Bum-bad-a-bum, bum-bad-a-bum," chanted Mr. Keller, holding both hands to his temples. "Enough to drive you crazy."

Jonathan looked keenly at him. "So you're not actually using the original main bedrooms?" he asked.

"Heavens, no," said Mrs. Keller. "They're much nicer than the ones we're sleeping in—well, they would be, if they were all painted and fixed up, anyway, and if the warped floorboards were taken out and replaced. We're using smaller rooms that were built as the old servants' bedrooms. When we get the upstairs floor in shape, we're all going to move up there, and I'm going to make the room where Ernest and I sleep a sewing room, and David's bedroom will be Ernest's office."

"Indeed," said Uncle Jonathan. "And how soon do you hope to move?"

"By the end of next month, or by the first week of November, anyway," Mrs. Keller said. "More meatballs, Jonathan?"

Later, as they drove back to town, Jonathan sighed. "You know, when Mrs. Keller talked about moving upstairs to sleep, I felt just exactly as though a goose had walked across my grave."

"Were you scared?" asked Lewis.

Uncle Jonathan grimaced, making his red beard bristle. "No," he said slowly. "But I had the strong sense that bad magic was at work. I'd bet dollars to dumplings that when the Kellers change bedrooms—if they do—this mysterious whatzis is going to burst out and cause big problems. Lewis, we might as well face it. We're going to have to pull out all the stops to learn just what the trouble is and how to fix it. We only have until the last day of next month."

Lewis gazed out the window at the tree-lined tunnel that was High Street. Overhead, all the leaves had turned, so they were driving beneath a glorious scarlet, orange, and yellow canopy.

Dully, trying to hold in his fear, Lewis whispered, "Until Halloween."

CHAPTER 12

ROSE RITA'S GRAMPA ALBERT Galway lived on a quiet street not far from the center of town. Quiet, that is, except for the Galway house itself, because Grampa Galway loved to tinker and build things, and dozens of his fanciful and odd miniature windmills crowded his small front yard. As the wind vanes spun, they operated cranks and gears that made two tiny men in a rowboat paddle as if they were fleeing from the clacking mouth of a sperm whale. On another windmill, a cyclist with legs twice the length of his body pedaled an old-fashioned bicycle with a tiny little rear wheel and an enormous front wheel. Another one featured a determined farmer who wielded a wooden axe and tried to chop off a turkey's head—except at the last moment the turkey pulled his head away.

All of this made a clattering, squeaking, flapping racket that one neighbor compared to a bushel of apples rolling down the tin roof of an old barn. However, Grampa Galway was a friendly and skillful man, always ready to do a good turn for a neighbor, and the people in his neighborhood forgave him for all the noise, or at least they put up with it.

When Rose Rita and Lewis called on Grampa Galway on the last day of September, he greeted them warmly, found seats for them in his cramped but neatly kept living room, and he brewed himself an oversized cup of strong brown tea, with hot cocoa for Lewis and Rose Rita. "It's a pleasure to see you again," Grampa Galway said, beaming at his visitors. "What can I do for you today?"

Rose Rita had prepared a story. "Maybe nothing, Grampa," she said, "but we wanted to try anyway. Lewis and I are sort of doing a research project on the superstitions and ghost stories of Hawaii, and we can't find much in the library. We thought maybe you might be able to help us out."

"Hm!" exclaimed Grampa Galway. He was not a large man, and though he was in his eighties, his movements were quick as a cricket's. "Well, I've visited the islands more than a few times, if that helps. I've been to Pearl Harbor, near Honolulu in Oahu, and I've spent a few weeks on Maui and a little more on the big island of Hawaii itself. I've seen Mauna Loa spouting red-hot lava at midnight, and I've seen some beautiful deep green valleys with silver water-falls at their heads. And I've watched the native women dance the hula-hula, which is not the funny kind of dance the television comics make it out to be, but a performance of mystery and beauty."

Lewis took a gulp of his hot cocoa. "That's great," he said. "But do you know anything about what the Hawaiians believe about hauntings and ghosts and things like that?"

"Well, some," said Grampa Galway slowly. "I won't say I'm any kind of expert, though. What do you need to know, kids?"

"Anything to do with curses," replied Rose Rita. "And especially anything that might involve myste-rious ghostly armies marching along through the night, and drums."

"And volcanoes," put in Lewis.

Mr. Galway sat bent forward in his chair, his elbows on his knees and his hands clasped in front of him. "Well, now. That sounds mighty mysterious. I'll tell you some of the stories I've heard, and then you can see if they'll help you any with your research."

He folded his arms and dropped his chin down onto his chest and sat in a thoughtful posture for a few moments. Then he asked, "Do you know any-thing about Pele?"

Lewis shook his head, but Rose Rita piped up: "She was the goddess of volcanoes in Hawaiian mythology, wasn't she?"

"Bingo," said her grandfather, beaming. He held up a long, bony finger. "Except I don't know if I would say *was*. She is supposed to live in the crater of Kilauea, one of the most active volcanoes on earth, but she loves to travel. She's the goddess of fire and destruction. The old Hawaiians called her, let me see if I can remember it . . ." He frowned for a moment and then said slowly, "*Wahine ai honua*. The woman who devours the land."

Rose Rita had whipped out her notepad, and she asked her grandfather to spell out the phrase. She copied it down and said, "She sounds dangerous."

"You could say that. There's a highway on Honolulu where the darndest things happen, or so they tell me. Pele sends a ghostly dog that chases cars. It comes closer and closer and grows until it's as big as the car it's chasing—and people who see it go insane and run their cars off a cliff. Or sometimes a motorist will see a woman in a sarong—that's a kind of tropical dress, silky and colorful—standing beside the road. She never looks the same way to any two people. Sometimes she's a gorgeous young woman with black or even blond hair. Other times she's a wrinkled, bent-over old lady. Anyway, it's always Pele. And if a driver stops to pick her up, it's because Pele is unhappy with him. She rides along for a spell and usually gives the driver a warning to mend his ways."

Lewis squirmed. None of that seemed to fit what

had happened, and he started to say something, but Rose Rita shot him a quick look of warning, so he settled back to listen.

Grampa Galway ran a hand over his bald head and shifted uncomfortably in his chair. "Now, this is where you might think I'm a little off my rocker, because this happened to someone I knew, a buddy of mine when I was in the navy. Mind, this could all just be a yarn of his, but I don't think so, somehow. He borrowed somebody's old jalopy and was driving around trying to buy souvenirs from the Hawaiians, very cheap. He planned to resell them to his ship-mates for a profit, you see. Well, anyway, he picked up a woman beside that highway one night. She was an old woman, that time, with a round face about as wrinkled as a walnut. As she climbs into the passenger seat, my friend, he says, 'Hey, Grandma, do you or any of your people have some trinkets you want to sell? Yankee dollar for them!'

"Well, sir, she says to him, 'Give me a cigarette.' See, this was back when lots of the islanders smoked, and they were always after sailors for cigs. My buddy passed her a cigarette and said, 'There's some matches in—' and then he looked at her and just about drove off the road."

"Why?" croaked Lewis, his throat dry despite the cocoa.

Grampa Galway held his hand up, flat, with his palm toward his face. "Because she was holding up her hand like this, and the palm of it burned red-hot, and she used that as a lighter, pushing the cigarette tip against her skin. A second later, the whole car filled up with smoke, so thick that my buddy had to pull over to the side of the road and bail out. He thought the car had spontaneously combusted. He ran around and opened the passenger door to rescue the old lady. Trouble was, no old lady was there. Nobody was there. Pele had just vanished away, like smoke herself."

"W-was he okay?" asked Lewis in a small voice.

"Hard to say," replied Grampa Galway, a distant look on his face. "Car wouldn't start. He had to spend all night out there, and when other vehicles zipped past, it was like the drivers couldn't even see him. Come daylight, he hiked a long way back, and after five miles or so, he met a Hawaiian man who was just standing beside the road. Man says, 'Pele does not like those who take away what belongs on her island, or those who cheat her sons and daughters.' My buddy finally caught a lift and came straight back to the ship and refused to get off again. That was the end of his souvenir business."

"That's interesting," murmured Rose Rita as she made a note in her pad, although Lewis thought it was horrible. He could imagine a hulking, gray-haired old woman lurching toward him in the night, her hands clenched into claws, reaching for him and bursting into fire as she came close.

106

"Is—is Pele still worshipped as a goddess?" asked Lewis.

"Who knows?" asked Grampa Galway. "Most of the Hawaiians I talked to seemed to think of her more as a kind of guardian spirit, the soul of the volcano, so to speak. Don't get me wrong. They don't all fear her or think she is evil. Just the opposite, in fact. Many of them look on her as a kind of supernatural grandmother, you might say, a being who protects and looks after them. They say she's very jealous, though. You don't dare take even a lump of volcanic rock from Hawaii, because if you do, Pele will punish you sooner or later."

"What about the other thing?" asked Rose Rita. "The whatchamacallits, the drum-beating ghosts?"

"Night Marchers," said Grampa Galway promptly. "*Huaka'i Po,* I've heard them called." He spelled out the words for Rose Rita, then continued: "They're the spirits of great warriors. They usually patrol an area, like the Wai Lua Valley. They march when the moon and the sea and the stars are just right, and, being ghostly, they can pass right through solid walls. They say sometimes you can see them—they kind of glow with their own inner light—but sometimes they're just dim shapes that vanish away when you try to look toward them."

"They're not dangerous, are they?" asked Lewis anxiously.

Grampa Galway glanced at him and hesitated for

a moment before answering. "Dangerous, Lewis? I don't know how to answer that, exactly. I know this much: When the Hawaiians build their houses, it's very important for them to know where the Night Marchers habitually walk. You see, if a house is accidentally built across one of the Night Marchers' trails, it won't even faze them. They'll just come trooping along with their spears and shields and all, as if the house wasn't even there. But there *is* one big danger."

"And what is that?" asked Rose Rita.

Grampa Galway looked uncomfortable. "I don't want to give you kids the willies or anything. This is just superstition, you understand. Anyway, they say that if the builder of the house has placed his bed in the way of the Night Marchers, when they come through, the sleeper's soul is yanked right out of his body. In the morning, the shell of the person is lying there in bed, unharmed but dead. And his soul—well, his soul is forced to travel with the Night Marchers forever until the end of time."

CHAPTER 13

"T HE ANCIENT HAWAIIANS DID not celebrate Halloween," insisted Uncle Jonathan as he and Lewis sat alone in the parlor of the house at 100 High Street. "So don't let that prey on your mind."

It was a blustery Sunday evening, and the next day was the last Monday in October. Lewis had felt a rising dread since their talk with Grampa Galway. He and Rose Rita had told Uncle Jonathan and Mrs. Zimmermann the whole story, and since then they had been concentrating on trying to learn more about Pele and the Night Marchers—but without much luck.

Lewis felt a growing fear of what might soon happen. "Next week is when the Kellers are going to move upstairs," he said. "What if that's where the Night Marchers go? Maybe David will be in the very same room where Princess Makalani died. And it's the time when regular ghosts and goblins are supposed to walk too, so something awful might happen."

Jonathan nodded. "I know, Lewis. But we have at least a little time yet, and now Florence knows what to research, so don't lose your head. Hum! I wish I could figure out a way to get into that place and give it a really good going-over."

In the weeks since their talk with Grampa Galway, Lewis had asked David about ghostly armies, but he had only frightened his friend. Rose Rita said she knew what was going on. "Pele brings the army to reclaim important stuff that was taken away from her island," she had argued. "What could be more important than a princess?"

"But the princess died years and years ago!" Lewis had insisted.

"Maybe," Rose Rita had suggested, "her spirit is still here!"

But Uncle Jonathan thought that Abediah Chadwick might have taken something else, some idol or relic, that Pele wanted. Now he insisted, "There must be *something* still left in the house that's causing all this uproar. If we could remove the whatever-it-is, maybe destroy it, we might lift the curse."

"I don't want you to go in there again!" said Lewis

wildly. He had a morbid fear of his uncle dying and leaving him alone in the world. What would he do then? He had few other relatives, and he didn't like any of them enough to want to go live with them. Even worse, his life would be one continual agony if he believed that his uncle's soul had been snatched by a ghostly parade and forced to join their eternal march.

"I'll be careful, whatever I do," replied his uncle reassuringly. At that moment the old grandfather clock off in the study whirred and gonged ten times, making a sound like a trunk full of tin plates falling solemnly and slowly down a flight of stairs, and Uncle Jonathan looked startled. He pulled out his pocket watch and double-checked the time. "Ten o'clock, and tomorrow is a school day! You'd better turn in, Lewis. And don't worry. I promise I won't lose my head and do anything silly."

Lewis usually loved his room. It had its own fireplace, where on chilly nights glowing embers made a sort of night-light, warm and friendly. Lewis had always liked his big, old-fashioned bed, with its headboard and footboard made of dark wood carved to resemble the battlements of a castle, and he had the luxury of shelf after shelf of old books to choose as bedtime reading.

On that Sunday night, though, everything in the room seemed vaguely wrong. An apprehensive Lewis took no book to bed with him, and as he lay sleepless, he twitched and flinched at each crackle of an ember in the fireplace. The flickering, ruddy light from the fire made shifting red patterns on the ceiling, reminding Lewis of the volcanic fountains shimmering in the mirror, of the fiery mask of a face he had glimpsed, and of the stolen pearl thrown by Potsworth Stevenson, bursting into a comet-like flare as it flew through the twilight. Every time Lewis closed his eyes, he seemed to hear a distant, threatening drumming. He would feel sweaty and panicky until he identified the source of the sound. Sometimes it was just the wind tap-tapping a shrub against the house, and other times it was his own heartbeat. The glowing dial of Lewis's bedside Westclox alarm clock kept telling him the hour was growing later. Eleven o'clock. Midnight. One in the morning.

Finally Lewis slipped into a fitful sleep. He began to dream. In the dream, he and Rose Rita were eleven years old again, and they were walking down the overgrown lane toward the Hawaii House. Lewis felt a leaden weight on his heart, because he had that creepy sensation called déjà vu, the feeling that he had already been here and lived through this and knew, or almost knew, what was going to happen next.

In the dream, somehow he and Rose Rita arrived at the house without having traveled all the way down the lane. They stood outside, looking up at the bleary, grimy windows. Rose Rita silently pointed, and following her gesture with his eyes, Lewis saw a window on the top floor slowly, slowly opening. It was the second window to the left of the tower and its open platform, where a terrified Abediah Chadwick had frozen to death rather than face what was behind the barricaded door.

Lewis wanted to turn and run, but he couldn't move his legs at all. He looked down. Somehow solid rock had grown up from the earth and enclosed his feet. He was frozen in place, like a statue on a pedestal. He looked at Rose Rita and wanted to shriek. She had been turned completely to stone, with one arm raised and blindly pointing.

Fragments of prayers he had learned as an altar boy flitted through his mind: *Ab insídiis diaboli, líbera nos, Dómine*—"From the assaults of the devil, good Lord deliver us." He tried to speak them aloud, but his jaws had locked. The window above opened fully, and he saw movement within. A sad-faced woman with long black hair gazed down at him. Then she beckoned him with her finger.

Somehow without consciously moving, Lewis found himself inside the Hawaii House, his feet free of the clutching stone. He was in the parlor with the shelves of knickknacks. Some of them had come to life. He saw them squirm and writhe all around him. A grotesque carved mask opened and closed its mouth, revealing triangular teeth like a shark's. On the deck of a model schooner, tiny sailors climbed the rigging and worked at the sails.

Somehow, though, when Lewis looked directly at a shelf, nothing on it moved. Then he was climbing a narrow, dark staircase. He pushed through a door into a hallway, and through another door that led to a bedroom. The dusty window was wide open, and through it he could see the immobile form of Rose Rita below, stone eyes staring sightlessly up, stone finger pointing silently. The woman who had been here had vanished, like a puff of steam—or a ghost.

The drums began to pound, not faint but loud and close by, and Lewis whirled. Through the wall came a shadowy, shoulder-hunched gray form, striding forward. Behind marched another, and another, and another—it was as if the wall had vanished, and Lewis could see an unending line of them, to the world's edge and beyond. The lead marcher was a fierce-looking warrior in loincloth, a feathered cloak, and a crested helmet, and he carried a wooden spear shaped like a javelin. Lewis retreated until his back thudded into the wall—he had nowhere to run—the point of the spear thrust into his chest—

He rolled right out of bed and woke as he tumbled to the floor, and for a moment he could not bring himself to realize that he was safe in his own room and that the marching ghosts were just part of a nightmare. The loud sound he heard was not the doom-laden drumbeat of the marchers, but his alarm clock. He must have thrashed around in his sleep and knocked it off, because it lay facedown on the bed, its bell muffled to a rat-tat-tat sound.

Lewis shakily untangled his legs from the sheets and stood up. He heard the lash of rain against the window and saw gray light outside. He picked up the clock. It was time for him to get up and go to school.

As he bathed and dressed, Lewis kept feeling as if he were on the deck of a ship at sea. The floor beneath his feet seemed to lift and fall, and his head spun from sleepiness. He debated what he should say to Uncle Jonathan, or if he should even say anything. After all, a dream couldn't really hurt you, and Uncle Jonathan would probably chalk it up to their talk with Grampa Galway.

When he was ready, Lewis tiptoed down the front stair. He slipped quietly into the dining room, where Uncle Jonathan already sat reading the newspaper and eating a bowl of Cheerios and some burnt-looking toast. He was a rotten cook, but he never liked to admit that, and whenever Uncle Jonathan fouled up a recipe, he usually ate the mess, while stubbornly insisting that it was delicious. "Good morning," he said to Lewis. "Good if you happen to be a duck or a tadpole, that is. Maybe I'd better drive you to school today, so you don't arrive looking like Jonah just after the great fish spewed him up on the shores of Mesopotamia."

Lewis grunted. He took down a bowl and poured

cereal and milk into it. He got a glass of orange juice to drink. Sliding into his usual chair at the table, he tried hard to look as if everything were normal.

Uncle Jonathan sipped his coffee and gazed silently at his nephew for a few moments. "Want the funny papers?" he asked, passing the newspaper across the table.

"Thanks." Lewis thumbed through the paper as he ate, stopping at the comics section.

Uncle Jonathan shook his head. "All right. Come clean. What's wrong with you?"

Lewis blinked. "What makes you think something's wrong?"

"For one thing, you're trying to read the adventures of Dick Tracy and the Phantom upside down. For another, you look like you just went a couple of rounds in the ring with Rocky Marciano." Marciano was a champion heavyweight boxer, and Lewis couldn't even imagine trying to trade blows with him.

"All this business with the Hawaii House is making it hard for me to sleep," he confessed.

"I know what you mean," Uncle Jonathan said. "Finish your breakfast and we'll break out the foul-weather gear and set off in the teeth of the roaring gale." He put his thumbs in the lower pockets of his vest and pushed back from the table, reciting:

The skipper hauled at the heavy sail:
"God be our help!" he only cried,

116

> As the roaring gale, like the stroke of a flail,
>   Smote the boat on its starboard side.

Lewis flinched as the wind outside howled and smote the Barnavelt house like a flail, or at least like a cat-o'-nine-tails. Jonathan said mildly, "That's literature, you know. It's a poem called 'The Wreck of Rivermouth,' by old John Greenleaf Whittier."

"Is it?" asked Lewis in a small voice.

"We used to have to memorize poetry by the ream when I was in school," murmured Jonathan. Behind his bushy, white-streaked red beard, he smiled. "Do they make you memorize them nowadays? Do you know Oliver Wendell Holmes's 'Old Ironsides'?"

Lewis drank the last of his orange juice and nodded.

"Let's say it together as we drive to school," suggested Uncle Jonathan. "That's a fine poem of anger and defiance, and I think we need a little of both right now!"

So they drove through whipping curtains of ferocious gray rain, reciting the poem that Oliver Wendell Holmes had written when some politicians wanted to scrap the famous old warship *U.S.S. Constitution*. It began with the ringing words:

> Aye, tear her tattered ensign down,
>   Long has it waved on high,
> And many an eye has danced to see
>   That banner in the sky!

When Uncle Jonathan pulled the car up in front of the school, he put a hand on Lewis's shoulder, stopping him from getting out into the storm for a moment. "Lewis," he said, "I want you to remember something. When Oliver Wendell Holmes wrote that poem in 1830, everyone was sure that Old Ironsides was going to be torn to pieces. But here it is more than a hundred years later, and do you know what? Old Ironsides is still floating in Boston Harbor, and she's still part of the navy. And now we face trouble too, but we are going to see this thing through. And at the end of it, David and his family are going to be in safe waters. Now, run and try not to drown before you can get inside!"

Lewis did. The cold rain stung his face and blatted against his yellow slicker, but somehow he felt a little more hopeful about weathering his own storm of fear and worry.

CHAPTER 14

WHILE THE GALE HOWLED outside, school dragged on. Rose Rita had a study period with David, and since she was one of those people who always did their studying days ahead of time, she didn't have to work hard to catch up, the way some kids did. She saw with alarm that David looked worse than ever. She had briefly spoken to Lewis just after they both arrived at school, and Lewis had also appeared strained and tense, with red eyes and a drooping, tired expression.

David was ten times worse. His face was as lined as a little old man's, and his red-rimmed eyes darted back and forth like two animals trapped in shallow, dark caves. Even the bullies were leaving him alone these days—he looked so beat-up that maybe they were afraid they'd get blamed for fighting with him.

The teacher in the study hall had a habit of waiting until the students had begun to read their texts or scribble in their notebooks, then strolling down to the teachers' lounge for a cup of coffee. As soon as she left, Rose Rita turned around and spoke to David, who sat at the desk behind her: "Are you all right?"

David nodded, but his lower lip quivered, and he blurted, "N-no!" He gasped for air, then jerked his head toward a table in the far back corner of the room, where students sat to work on group projects. He picked up his math book and headed back to the table, and Rose Rita got her own book and followed him. By then nobody was paying much attention, anyway. As soon as the teacher had gone, everyone started talking and joking, just quietly enough so that the next-door teacher wouldn't hear and come in to scold them.

Under cover of the buzz and rustle of all those conversations, David opened his math book and bent down over it. Rose Rita sat across from him and opened her book too. "What's up?" she asked in little more than a whisper.

David had to try several times before he could speak. "D-do you buh-believe in guh-ghosts?" he stammered. "B-b-because I, I really do think our h-h-house is huh-haunted."

Rose Rita felt a pang inside. She remembered

some terrifying times—the ghostly figure that Lewis had accidentally summoned once when his uncle gave him a lucky three-cent piece, the terrible haunted opera house where an evil spirit had cast a spell to enslave the world, and other bad memories. "I have to," she said. "I've sort of seen some."

David's face contorted as he began to spill out the reasons for his question. He started with Uncle Jonathan's remark, went on to the things Lewis had hinted at, and wound up with things he had seen and heard. Rose Rita had to listen hard, and sometimes he had to repeat himself. She followed the drift, though.

As Mr. Keller had repaired the floors of the upstairs bedrooms, the sound of the night drums had grown worse. Though not much more than painting remained to be done in the rooms, now Mr. Keller would never spend more than half an hour upstairs. Complaining that the paint fumes were too strong, he would come back down and rest, but as often as not he would decide not to go back up. This was not like David's father, who always said that you should plan a job so that you could work at it and finish it as soon as possible. David said he thought his father looked scared after these episodes. "H-he h-h-hears things up th-there," David said urgently.

His mother was losing sleep too, and she and Mr. Keller were having bitter arguments about money late at night. David was beginning to hate going to bed.

If he didn't hear the sounds of his parents' angry voices, he heard the pounding of those drums.

When David finished, Rose Rita was silent for a few moments. Then she asked, "Have you *seen* anything?"

"Men," David said. "An a-army of m-men."

When the storm blew itself out that afternoon, the autumn leaves lay strewn and soggy on the ground, and the trees reached bare, skeletal fingers up toward the clearing sky. Rose Rita spoke to Lewis, and what she had to say dismayed him.

"I can't!" he said in despair as they walked past sodden lawns and streaming gutters.

"You'll have to," said Rose Rita urgently. "I certainly can't go to David's house for a sleepover. He wants someone else to see and hear these things, just so he'll know he isn't losing his mind. The Kellers know they sort of owe you one, because of how your uncle has helped them. If David asks his mom and dad if you can come and spend the night this coming Friday, they'll say yes. Look, Lewis, you've got to get up the nerve for this. I know it's a lot to ask—"

"Don't rub it in," moaned Lewis. "I hate being a coward."

"You're not," insisted Rose Rita. "You have plenty of reason to be afraid. But you know what a hero is? It's someone who's afraid and still does what he has to do, that's all."

"But what am I supposed to do?"

"Maybe Mrs. Zimmermann can tell us."

They walked to her house beneath a sky of flying, broken clouds, buffeted by increasingly chilly gusts of wind. It looked as if a real cool spell was moving in, a taste of winter days ahead. Rose Rita knocked on the door, and Mrs. Zimmermann answered it almost at once. She must have been in the parlor already. "My goodness," she said. "Come in, you two. You look as glum as a gib-cat!"

"What's that?" asked Rose Rita.

"To tell the truth, I don't know!" responded Mrs. Zimmermann with a chuckle. "Shakespeare mentions it in one of his plays—*Henry IV*, I think. 'As melancholy as a gib-cat,' it goes, and though I don't know what one is, that's the way you look. Sit down and tell me what the trouble is. More supernatural goings-on at the Hawaii House?"

"Yes," said Rose Rita, and she quickly explained what David had told her and what she had asked Lewis to do.

Mrs. Zimmermann listened solemnly. Then she gave Lewis a keen, knowing glance. "I'd say the decision is up to Lewis, but it may be a good idea. I have spent a lot of time driving to universities and calling people who study folklore and mythology."

"We tried to research that too," said Lewis. "But the trouble is, our school library has hardly anything about Hawaii at all, except in the encyclopedias, and the public library just has two travel books."

"Information is sort of hard to come by," admitted Mrs. Zimmermann. "However, I have found out a few things that have me caught betwixt and between, as they say down South. Did any of the encyclopedias or books you found mention Kamehameha?"

Lewis looked at Rose Rita, and she stared blankly back at him. "No," they said almost together.

"It ties in to the Hawaii House, but in a kind of complicated way. Anyhow, Kamehameha was the first king to unite all of the Hawaiian Islands under one rule. He was born at a time when the islands had four different quarreling kings. He became a respected warrior, and during one of his battles, the volcano sacred to Pele erupted and destroyed so many of his enemies that Kamehameha's army won a great victory. The people decided that meant Pele was on his side.

"Well, to make a long story short, before 1800, Kamehameha became the single king of all the Hawaiian people. The Hawaiians think of him the way we think of George Washington and Abraham Lincoln put together."

"That's all very interesting," said Rose Rita. "But what does he have to do with the Hawaii House?"

Mrs. Zimmermann laughed. "Heavens, Rose Rita, you get right to the point. Well, the short answer again is this: Makalani was distantly related to Kamehameha. She truly had royal blood in her veins. Now, I think she fell deeply in love with Abediah Chadwick, and I believe he loved her. But I can guess at what must have happened. One of her relatives on the islands resented her running away with an American sailor, even if he was a wealthy man. That relative, whoever he or she was, appealed to Pele."

"It's a kind of curse, then," Lewis said.

"Exactly so," replied Mrs. Zimmermann. "When people took anything, even a fragment of hardened lava, from Pele's islands, she saw to it that they had plenty of misery unless they returned it. Now it appears that Pele—or some force, anyway—has sent ghostly warriors to patrol the Hawaii House. They can be dangerous, as you very well know, but one thing they *can't* do is to retrieve solid objects. Like all ghosts, they are insubstantial and pass right through ordinary matter, the way we pass through air."

"Then how do they kill people?" asked Rose Rita.

In a resigned voice, Mrs. Zimmermann said, "I am an expert in magic amulets and talismans, Rose Rita, not a student of the unnatural history of ghosts. I imagine that they separate the spirits of the living from their bodies in some way, and without the spirit, the body perishes. Anyway, if, and it is a big if, we could discover just what the Marching Dead are trying to find or retrieve, we would stand a good chance of being able to help David and his family."

"Isn't there another way?" asked Lewis.

"Who knows? There may well be, but I haven't come across any. Oh, I wish there were some fool-proof, easy way to put an end to our doubts and our suspicions, but there isn't. At any rate, we members of the Capharnaum County Magicians Society have sworn not to allow any evil magic to operate in our territory, and—"

Someone pounded on the door, and everyone jumped a foot. Mrs. Zimmermann rose from her armchair, but a moment later the door opened and Uncle Jonathan poked his head in. "I thought you two might be here," he said to Lewis. "What's this? A meeting of the Committee to Chase Out Haunts, Ghoulies, and Ghosties without me?"

"Oh, come in, Fat Ears," said Mrs. Zimmermann tartly. "We were trying to work out a plan to take a peek inside the top floor of the Kellers' house."

"I still think I should volunteer to help out with the painting," said Uncle Jonathan.

"You'd be too busy to do any good," replied Mrs. Zimmermann. "Besides, we have already fouled things up once. No, we have an alternative—but it will mean that Lewis will be the one who must look around."

Lewis felt as if a chill hand had just clutched him

around the neck. Mrs. Zimmermann continued, "Of course, we plan to be close by. I can arrange things so the amulet will give us a warning if anything serious begins to happen. The crystal in my umbrella handle will flash and flare."

"And we'll come riding to the rescue," put in Uncle Jonathan. "Armed to the teeth with protective spells and loaded for bear."

Rose Rita lowered her gaze and bit her lip. Lewis knew what she must be thinking: She would be brave enough to venture into the house alone. Only a girl couldn't go on a sleepover at a boy's house, so she couldn't do it. None of them could, except for him. Lewis had the sensation, miserable and lonely, of being on the verge of letting them all down.

Uncle Jonathan gave Lewis a quick glance. "Lewis, we can try to figure some other way if you're not up to this, and we won't think any the less of you. Tell me, do you want to go through with this plan?"

Lewis was taking deep breaths. "No, I don't," he confessed. He couldn't help remembering how bad David had looked in their classes together, or the story Rose Rita had told about the things he had heard and seen. Lewis knew exactly how David felt, trapped and hopeless. And if he were in David's place, Lewis knew how badly he would want someone's help. "I don't want to," Lewis continued, "but I think I have to."

Uncle Jonathan gazed at him for a long, long

moment. "Lewis," he said softly, in a strangely choked voice, "I am so proud of you."

Despite his fears, Lewis felt his heart swell with warmth and pride. He would risk anything—even anything the Hawaii House could throw at him—for his uncle's words of praise and admiration.

CHAPTER 15

FRIDAY AFTERNOON, THE DAY before Halloween, was clear and unseasonably cold. Everything had been arranged with the Kellers, and Uncle Jonathan dropped Lewis off at five. Lewis carried his gym bag with a change of clothes. Under his shirt, where no one could see, he was wearing something Mrs. Zimmermann had given him. It was a powerful protective amulet on a thin gold chain. The magical item looked a little like the orb on Mrs. Zimmermann's umbrella: a small crystal ball, about half the size of a marble, with a faint purple light lurking inside it.

"This is very ancient," Mrs. Zimmermann had confided to him. "It dates from 1050 B.C. and once decorated the hilt of a mystic sword. It's belonged to scads of good magicians over the years, and at last it fell into the hands of a descendant of the Knights Templar, one of my teachers when I studied magic. He gave it to me when I was still a student at the University of Göttingen, and I have kept it safe ever since."

"What is it?" Lewis had asked.

With a wink, Mrs. Zimmermann replied, "Nothing at all but a sphere of quartz crystal, Lewis. Now, some people believe that some crystals send out super-duper vibrations that give good health and prosperity and so on. That simply is not true. But then, this particular crystal sphere has absorbed years and years of good influences, and many great and kindly sorcerers have cast beneficent spells on it. I don't think even Pele herself could do harm to you as long as that little gem stays around your neck. And thanks to a little hocus-pocus of my own, it will also prove to be a guide to what we need to find."

Lewis nodded. He trusted Mrs. Zimmermann, but—well, he *really* hoped her spells would work.

Friday afternoon came, and as he stood on the veranda of the Hawaii House, Lewis secretly touched the crystal globe hanging inside his shirt. He sent up a silent prayer asking for protection and freedom from fear and noticed as he did that he could see the vapor of his breath rising up like a soul heading for heaven. When Mrs. Keller opened the door, he steeled himself and gave her the best smile he could manage. David greeted him, and they sat at the dining room table playing checkers while Mrs. Keller cooked dinner.

Ernest Keller dragged home from his job at the post office at five thirty. He mumbled a tired greeting and sank with a grateful-sounding sigh into a chair at the end of the table. He didn't talk much as he watched David wipe the floor with Lewis at checkers, pulling off a spectacular triple jump that left him with three red kings and Lewis with one lonely pursued black checker. When David cornered Lewis's last checker, Mr. Keller gave his son a smile. "Good game, boys," he said, looking as if he were trying to hold in a yawn.

David said quietly, "Thanks, Dad," not stumbling over either word.

Uncle Jonathan must have mentioned to Mr. Keller that he and Lewis were Catholic, Lewis thought, because for dinner Mrs. Keller served baked salmon, along with mixed vegetables and rice. Catholics were not supposed to eat meat on Fridays, but fish was allowed. It was a good, solid meal, and afterward, David and Lewis washed and dried the dishes, earning a weary "Thank you, boys," from Mrs. Keller. The Kellers did not have a TV set, but Mr. Keller sat in a threadbare armchair in the parlor and listened to a boxing match on the radio, while Mrs. Keller settled down on the sofa, turned on a table lamp, and began to read a book. Lewis and David sat on the floor on either side of the coffee table and switched from checkers to chess. David wasn't very good at that, so Lewis, who was an experienced if not great player, talked him through the game, showing him how to anticipate possible moves and traps.

However, Lewis wasn't an entirely attentive chess instructor that evening. His nerves were too strained, and his attention strayed so that he gave David bad advice and made some foolish moves. He spent every moment straining to hear the sound of drums. Outside the Hawaii House, deep night fell. At nine o'clock Mrs. Keller drew the curtains over those tall windows, but Lewis could feel the weight of darkness outside, pressing down on the house, pressing in on it. Somewhere out there his friends waited in Uncle Jonathan's old car, perhaps sharing a thermos of hot cocoa or playing Twenty Questions to while away the time.

Lewis looked longingly out into the night as Mrs. Keller closed the curtains on all the windows. As his ears listened for the sound of drums, his restless eyes strayed over the tall shelves and the memorabilia displayed on them. "Still got all this stuff, huh?" he asked.

David nodded. The two of them looked over the collection on the shelves: ships and seashells, carvings and models, sextants and bo's'n whistles. As David said, "I th-think this is wh-what the sailors used to f-find their location," Lewis pressed his finger against the amulet he wore, but he felt nothing.

He took the old brass sextant and looked at its array of lenses and mirrors. "I don't know how to use one of these," he said.

David shrugged. "I don't either."

When it was time for bed, Lewis found that the Kellers had set up a folding army cot in David's room for him. Even though the bedroom had been intended for a servant, it was a big one, larger even than Lewis's room, and a wide expanse of wood floor separated the cot from David's bed against the opposite wall.

The cot had been shoved against the wall beneath the room's one window. Lewis got ready for bed, going into the bathroom between David's room and his parents' to change into his blue and gray diamond-patterned pajamas and carefully buttoning the jacket to hide the amulet.

David sat on the edge of his bed and asked, "Wh-what are you up to, L-Lewis? Really?"

He looked so upset that Lewis didn't have the heart to lie. "Don't be scared," he said softly. "Listen: My uncle and Mrs. Zimmermann want to help you. They think you're right about this house. It's—it's, well, kind of haunted."

David's bloodshot eyes got round. "I knew it," he whispered. "Are y-your uncle and Mrs. Z-Zimmermann gh-ghost hunters?"

"In a way." Lewis didn't want to spill all their secrets, but he did add, "They know that sometimes weird things are real, weird things that most people don't believe in. They think the noises and the things you've seen are caused by something that the man who built this house left here. Tonight they want me to go looking for it."

"D-do I h-have to come?" asked David apprehensively.

Lewis gulped down his fear. "No. I'll call you if I need you." David fell silent, and as Lewis lay there, he heard plenty of noises. The old house settled, its timbers creaked and groaned. A lonesome whip-poor-will called over and over from outside. With the lights out, the window above Lewis's cot glowed a faint blue from the light of the rising moon.

Louis lay with his eyes open, determined not to nod off. "Whatever you do," Uncle Jonathan had warned, "don't go to sleep. And try to slip upstairs before midnight if you can, or if you can't, wait until one o'clock or later. No sense taking chances by going just at the witching hour."

David sighed and muttered, but eventually his breathing fell into a regular rhythm. The pale green dial of his bedside clock said that it was ten minutes past eleven. Cautiously, Lewis swung his legs off the cot and got to his feet.

The wood floor felt hard and splintery beneath Lewis's bare feet. He found his sneakers in the dark and slipped them on. He pulled the laces tight and tied them, then brought his feet down slowly and softly to keep the rubber soles from squeaking on the wood. David had not fully closed the bedroom door, and Lewis opened it inch by inch, not daring to push too hard in case the hinges groaned. He could hear muffled snoring coming from David's parents' room down past the bathroom. He had to go in the opposite direction.

"Sst!" The whisper made Lewis leap in fright, his heart hammering.

Behind him, David was sitting up in bed. Lewis could see his wide eyes gleaming in the faint light. "Shh," Lewis warned him.

"Wh-where are y-you going to search?"

Lewis stepped back into the room and leaned against the wall. "Second floor. I have to see if I can find anything that's causing the—the trouble," he whispered. "Want to change your mind and help me?"

David whimpered, and Lewis saw him sink back onto the bed. "It's okay," Lewis said softly. He forced himself to walk through the doorway, as difficult a step as he had ever taken.

Into the darkened hall, with one hand on the wall to guide him, past the parlor, and then down the far hall to the stair. A twenty-five-watt bulb, hardly brighter than a night-light, burned halfway up at the landing, leaving the stairway below and above it in a dim half-illumination. Lewis held his breath as he climbed, praying that the amulet worked, that whatever lurked in the house would have no power over him. At the top of the stair, Lewis felt a shivery tingle. This was familiar to him. He had been here before—in that bad dream. At least Rose Rita wasn't standing outside, petrified into stone.

But he didn't know which door led into the bedroom from which the woman in that dream had beckoned to him. He opened one of the two doors and in the faint spill of light leaking in from the landing below, he found another short flight of stairs leading upward to a closed door. Across from him, at the foot of this stair, he could barely make out another doorway.

The short stair had to be the way up to the tower platform. That was the only part of the house it could possibly lead to. At the top of these stairs was the way out onto the open floor where Abediah Chadwick had frozen to death, afraid to return to the warmth of the house because *something* horrible was on the other side of the door.

Lewis clutched the amulet under his pajama jacket. He stood for a moment on the landing, then opened the other door leading off the stairwell. A sharp scent of house paint stung his nostrils. He jerked in alarm as he saw a looming figure in the darkness, shrouded and glowing palely white in the moonlight streaming through the uncurtained windows. The monstrous shape had a flattened head, like the Frankenstein monster in the old movies, and it stood absolutely still, as still as a cat whose narrowed eyes had caught sight of a helpless mouse. With an effort, Lewis stifled a scream.

And a moment later, he went limp with relief. The grim apparition was—nothing more than a stepladder, covered with a tarp, and a gallon bucket of paint stood balanced on the top step, providing the head.

Lewis found the old-fashioned light switch and pushed the top button. It moved reluctantly, sinking under his finger and giving off a dull click.

Nothing else happened. Either the bulbs were burned out, or the electricity in this room was not working. The darkness made everything Lewis had to do more difficult. The door behind him wanted to swing closed. Probably it was just badly balanced on its hinges, but Lewis couldn't shake off the nervous feeling that unseen creatures were trying to push the door shut to seal off the little light filtering in from the one dim bulb in the stairway.

Lewis felt around with his foot, searching for something to use to brace the door, but nothing lay within reach. He could dart over to the ladder, but the door would swing shut before he could grab the gallon of paint—and what if it locked itself? Possibly he could go downstairs and bring up something, but Lewis knew that once out of that room, he would never be able to get up the nerve to return to it. He knew what he had to do to find the source of the haunting—but he couldn't bring himself to try it with only the feeble moonlight to help. All he needed was something to jam beneath the door. He had a sudden inspiration, bent over, and tugged the bows of his sneakers. He pulled off his shoes. They would have to do.

He opened the door as wide as he could and tried to wedge the toe of one of the sneakers underneath, but the gap wasn't wide enough. Maybe the rubber soles would provide enough friction to hold the door open and let the anemic light in.

Lewis edged into the room, then reached under his collar and pulled out the amulet. As long as it was around his neck, Mrs. Zimmermann had said, he was safe. But now, following her instructions, he had to pull the chain over his head. He hoped with all his heart that just clutching the sphere would protect him. Holding the chain so the crystal hung straight down, he started to whisper the words that Mrs. Zimmermann had made him memorize, an ancient Latin incantation. If everything worked, if he was lucky—

He felt a sort of vibration coming through the gold chain. The almost undetectable purple star deep in the heart of the little orb pulsed like a tiny flickering Christmas bulb. Slowly, slowly, the crystal began to move, spinning in tight circles. The circles grew larger until the glowing ball was like a miniature model of the moon, orbiting round and round on the end of the gold chain.

The circle began to wobble. The circular movement changed to a side-to-side rocking. Incredibly, one side of the movement became more and more pronounced. The orb was defying gravity—it was pointing. It swung toward the sill of one of the two windows that looked out over the front lawn. It stood almost straight out now, pulling at the chain. Like a compass needle, like a divining rod, the globe seemed to be attracted to something, though he couldn't see anything there at all.

Lewis took two uncertain steps toward the spot that was attracting the amulet, feeling again the cold, hard wood beneath his feet. If only he had a little more light. He craved light the way a man lost in a desert might crave water. His whole soul thirsted for it.

He heard a whispery noise behind him—not the sound of drums, not the sound of breathing, but the soft swish of his shoes, slipping across the floor as the door slowly closed itself, cutting off the light from the stairwell.

Inches away from touching the wall, Lewis stood in tormented indecision. He did not want to be alone in that dark room. Yet he knew he had to follow the glowing orb's lead, or his mission would be a complete failure.

Breathing an almost silent prayer, Lewis took

another step forward, and another, his left hand holding the chain, his right outstretched to touch the window—

The chain felt different, the tug harder than he remembered.

Outside the world lay in darkness, except for the glow of a waning moon through the windows to his right and left. And in that glow Lewis saw that someone else was in the room. A hand grasped the chain, pulling it to one side, diverting the sphere from the direction it wanted to take. Lewis felt as if his insides had suddenly turned to ice, and he thought in a panicked way of the fate suffered by Abediah Chadwick.

Then something in the old, frayed electrical wiring somehow caught. He had left the light switch on, and now electricity started to flow with a barely audible buzzing. Two lightbulbs in a ceiling globe flickered into spectral orange life, weak as a single birthday candle.

The hand pulling the amulet was slim, a woman's hand, with pale, oval-shaped nails, a young hand.

And it floated in midair, unattached to an arm.

CHAPTER 16

I CAN'T STAND THIS," GRUMBLED Uncle Jonathan.

"Oh, hush," snapped Mrs. Zimmermann, though her tone was as worried as Jonathan's. "It's not even midnight yet, and my wand isn't showing the least trace of a warning. Lewis is fine."

Rose Rita sat in the backseat of the old Muggins Simoon and wished that she were as sure as Mrs. Zimmermann sounded. She knew Lewis very well, and she admired him in many ways. However, Rose Rita had a level head and a clear way of thinking. She knew that Lewis was likely to panic in sticky situations, and she had often heard his worry-wart mutterings about his many obscure fears and phobias. She practically itched to fly to his aid in some way, even though she knew she couldn't.

Her mother and father would have been shocked and alarmed if they had any inkling of what they were up to. The two of them knew that Rose Rita was spending the night with Mrs. Zimmermann—"She needs me to help her with some things," Rose Rita had said, not untruthfully. They did *not* know that Mrs. Zimmermann and Uncle Jonathan were on a sort of ghostly stakeout, as the police show *Dragnet* on TV called this sort of waiting and watching. The old car stood parked in the last curve of the long driveway with its lights out and its engine off. Before them, framed by the black backdrop of the woods, the Hawaii House lay bathed in the pallid light of a waning moon.

Uncle Jonathan had muttered about that. "Nearly last quarter," he had complained. "Why couldn't it have been a full moon? A quarter-moon brings changes."

"I know all about sky magic, Frazzle Face," returned Mrs. Zimmermann. "What do you expect me to do about it, though? I can't say *abracadabra* and make the moon shine full and bright. On the other hand, you just might be able to work up your whammy and cause a magical eclipse, but unless I miss my guess, we're all agreed that the last thing we want is a truly pitch-dark night."

After such minor disagreements, they had settled in, and to Rose Rita it seemed that hours had crept by, slowly, on hands and knees. Mrs. Zimmermann produced some cold chicken sandwiches and a thermos of hot cocoa, and they had dined in the dark. The pleasant aroma of the food filled the car, but enjoying it was impossible when worry clenched Rose Rita's throat. The chicken turned to an unappetizing mush in her mouth. Even the sweet, rich cocoa felt as if it stopped somewhere short of her stomach.

Then, as her eyelids began to feel as if they had been dipped in sand, Mrs. Zimmermann suddenly gasped. "Jonathan!"

Rose Rita craned forward to peer over the top of the front seat. Mrs. Zimmermann held her umbrella, point down toward the floor of the car, handle up. And the purple light inside the orb flashed, like the beacon of a lighthouse sending out its warning.

"Look!" Uncle Jonathan pushed open the driver's door and stepped out, and Rose Rita saw that a ruddy light outlined his figure. Two of the windows in the Hawaii House had blazed red. The crimson windows were to the left of the square tower with its exposed platform.

Mrs. Zimmermann was out too, and now Rose Rita leaped from the old car. "What's happening?"

Mrs. Zimmermann tapped her umbrella on the ground. Somehow it grew, extended itself into a tall staff, taller than Mrs. Zimmermann, and the globe flashed like a star being born. "Nothing harmful . . . I don't think," said Mrs. Zimmermann, her voice tight. "It's as if some ghostly presence has arrived, but I can't sense anger or hostility. I wish I knew just what—"

Something exploded in absolute silence. Rose Rita felt a wave of heat slam into her and shove her backward, and she staggered to keep her footing. Brilliant scarlet light dazzled her eyes, blinding her.

Drums pounded. A low, rhythmic guttural chant filled her ears. The ground trembled beneath her feet.

"*Avaunt!*" bellowed Uncle Jonathan, holding up his cane, an inky silhouette against a wavering billow of red light. "Let no evil thing come nigh!"

Mrs. Zimmermann held her staff straight before her, her arm stiff. Tears stung Rose Rita's eyes from the brightness of the blaze before them, a sheet of flame stretching from ground to sky. Its base was the intense orange of a bonfire, and as it rose, the sheet reached white-hot intensity. Looking at it felt like trying to squint into the fiery heart of a blast furnace. A hot wind rolled from the glare. It stirred Mrs. Zimmermann's hair. Somehow her baggy dress had transformed into the flowing robes of a powerful sorceress, their purple color so intense that staring at them, you got the feeling you were gazing into the heart of the universe. The rush of heated air billowed the garment out behind her in great rolling waves.

"Pele!" Mrs Zimmermann shouted. "Are you here?"

Darkness hit again like a silent peal of thunder,

and Rose Rita felt the whole world vibrate and quiver from the impact. Where was the house? She couldn't see it any longer. She reached out and felt the cool, reassuring touch of the car. She hadn't gone blind— the double glow from Uncle Jonathan's cane and Mrs. Zimmermann's staff still shone. But the house had vanished. What had happened?

"Who calls my name?"

Rose Rita squeaked in alarm. From the night a figure emerged, an imperious young woman dressed in silky red robes, with her long dark hair streaming, fluttering around her, as though touched by rising hot air. She strode forward. Her face was terrible and beautiful, and her flesh glowed with an inner light, as if fires burned just beneath her skin. Her eyes should have been dark, but the pupils glared like white-hot embers.

Uncle Jonathan's hand fell on Rose Rita's shoulder. "Let Florence handle this," he said in a soft voice. "She's the real McCoy."

Mrs. Zimmermann stepped forward, taller somehow. Dark red flames, giving no illumination, rolled up from the earth and surrounded the ghostly figure that had stopped ten feet away. Purple flames blossomed as Mrs. Zimmermann moved forward, tracing her path, then writhing around her figure. The two women stopped barely three feet from each other. "Pele?" asked Mrs. Zimmermann.

"I have come far," the other replied. "Why do you try to stop me?"

"You have no claim on these people," answered Mrs. Zimmermann. "I know the stories they tell of you: From island to island you traveled across the seas, seeking a home. Always when you found an inviting cavern it filled with water, until at last you came to rest in beautiful Hawaii. That is your home. That is where you should be."

"What is mine was taken," the other woman said. "A stranger came, a thief, and took something most dear to me. Shall I not reclaim my own?"

Mrs. Zimmermann stood tall, holding her staff before her. "You have taken more than that. You have taken innocent lives. You will take no more."

Pele's body blazed like a jetting fountain of molten lava. "You," said a voice like the rumble of an explosion, "are wrong, old woman." From the folds of her clothing, Pele held up a weapon, a paddle-like club, its edges spiked with sharp white teeth—except for one gap near the tip, where one of the teeth was missing. "This I claimed many years ago. Tonight I claim the rest, and you cannot stop me."

Rose Rita felt as if she, as if everything in the world were shrinking to nothing before the fiery anger of the great and fearsome figure standing before them. She felt Uncle Jonathan catch her arm. If he had not held her up, she would have collapsed from awe and despair. How would they, how *could* they fight this unearthly being?

Lewis held the chain in a death grip as the disembodied hand stubbornly tried to pull it away. With a flash, a crimson light flooded the room, turning everything red. Now Lewis could see the rest of the figure before him, a transparent gray silhouette. Her hand was the only solid part of her, but it clearly was the young woman who had beckoned to him from the window in his dream. "Stop it!" he said with a gasp. "Let go!"

The young woman nodded toward the door, her face showing urgency and concern. Lewis realized with a shock that she was trying to warn him—warn him to stop what he was doing and leave the room. "I—I want to help you," he said, his voice quavering in fear.

The ghostly grip loosened. The orb dropped. From the delicate oval fingernails, solidity flowed into the arm, the body and face of the figure. The young woman had a fine, proud face, jet-black hair, and a defiant thrust of her chin. She wore the old-fashioned clothes of the 1870s, a dress that might really be white but that looked red in the unearthly light filling the room. The woman's great wide eyes were dark with sorrow. "You cannot. Go, please. Just go."

The woman had not spoken. At least, Lewis had not seen her lips move. Still, a sweet voice seemed to echo in his head. "I have to," he said.

"You cannot. I have waited here for my husband.

His spirit cannot join mine. If you take what you wish to take, then Pele wins, and my spirit must go with her warriors. Leave it here. Leave this house. I had rather remain here for all eternity, close to my husband, than be taken halfway around the world from him."

Lewis understood. "You are Makalani."

"I am Makalani, daughter of kings, descended from Pele. Of my own choice I left my island and came here, and of my own will I remain."

"I want to help," said Lewis. "I'm only trying to help."

"It is too late! It begins again!"

Nothing shimmered or faded, the way things did in the movies, but somehow the brilliant light went away, and Lewis stood alone in the room. No. Not alone. A woman lay sleeping in a big bed, her dark hair spilled across the pillows. The lovely, calm face was Makalani's. On a small round table beside the bed a single candle burned, its flame pale and yellow. The door opened, and from the top landing a man stepped in, a tall man, his thick hair nearly white except right on top, where a dark wave of it lay brushed back from his forehead. Long white whiskers came down his cheeks. His eyebrows scowled fiercely above eyes as deep blue as the open Pacific, and his nose jutted out like the prow of a mighty ship. His expression softened as he gazed at the sleeping Makalani. Then he raised his arm, and Lewis cried out in shock.

The man—he had to be Abediah Chadwick, the wealthy ship owner who had married Makalani and brought her here—carried what was clearly a weapon. It looked something like a slender tennis racquet carved from some shiny red wood. In the edges of the paddle part, though, deadly white points gleamed in a sawtooth pattern. Shark's teeth. The thing was some sort of primitive weapon, a war club.

A sound of drums! The man said harshly, "They've found us, my love! They're coming!"

Makalani awoke instantly, rolling from the bed and standing beside her husband. She said something in a foreign language, something full of L's and R's and murmurous vowels. "I will try," the man replied.

The first warrior came through the wall next to the window closest to the head of the bed. Chadwick sprang forward, right *through* Lewis, who flinched and spun in the same moment. With a furious sweep of the war club, Chadwick struck at the armed figure. The warrior dissolved into mist, his body streaming as if a blast of wind had hit him.

Lewis backed against the wall, felt it hard and cool behind him. Chadwick faced a stream of marching warriors, grim in their helmets and armor. Chadwick struck again, but though each warrior he hit vanished, there were too many of them. They crowded close, they tried to press past Chadwick to get at Makalani. The older man grunted with effort, the club a blur as he fought the ghostly army.

And then one of them hurled a javelin-like spear as he emerged. Chadwick swung wildly, missed the ghostly spear, and turned to see it pierce Makalani's heart. She gave one soft cry and fell back on the bed. "No!" shouted Chadwick. He furiously slashed at the warrior, whose body puffed away.

The drums ceased. From somewhere a woman's laughter, cold and cruel, broke out. Chadwick, his face streaming with tears, lifted Makalani's body. He put her back in the bed, gently put the covers over her, crossed her hands. Then he looked toward the windows. "You didn't get her," he said. "You released her spirit, but I kept the warrior from taking it. You won't get her as long as I can hold out. As long as I have something of yours!"

Drums. Louder.

A huge warrior burst through the wall. Chadwick leaped forward, bringing the club up from his knees, striking at the ghostly form. Thud! The club passed through the dissolving form of the warrior but then slammed into the underneath edge of the windowsill with such force that the window flew open. Chadwick pulled with desperate strength. One of the shark's teeth had penetrated the windowsill so deeply that half an inch or more stuck up through splintered wood. More warriors poured through, menacing Chadwick. Abandoning the jammed club, he retreated. He slammed the door, and Lewis heard his footsteps on the short stair leading up to the platform.

Now the warriors had faded. He heard chants from the stairwell, scrapes and creaks as Chadwick barricaded the platform door. Through the slightly open window air blasted in with the breath of ice. Lewis felt as though he were glued to the wall beside the bed.

Makalani somehow stood at the foot of her bed, even as her body lay there unmoving. And then another woman appeared, tall and fierce, her silky robes made of glowing red and orange fabric, flowers adorning her hair. "Child. All the others in the house have become part of my army of ghosts. Now I have come for you."

"I will not go."

"You belong to me."

"I belong with my husband."

"No. You are a child of the sun-sparkling sea and the high white clouds in a smiling blue sky. You are a child of the deep green valleys and the smoky streams of waterfalls. You are mine."

"I am my own."

The second woman—and Lewis could guess this was Pele—reacted with a snarl of rage. She grasped the war club and wrenched it from where it had stuck in the windowsill. Lewis heard a snap. For an instant a white chip stood out on the face of the dark night as the tip of the tooth fractured and flew off outside. Pele brandished the club, and Lewis could see the gap where one of the great shark's teeth had broken short. "This a man stole from a temple," said Pele. "This I take, as I shall take the sacred pearl stolen by another and given to the man who crossed the sea. As I shall take you."

"You will not take me," returned Makalani, defiance in her voice. "Not as long as my husband keeps watch!"

"So be it!"

The floor beneath Lewis's feet heaved. He fell heavily. The next instant he lay in darkness, not sure if he was conscious or unconscious, alive or dead.

CHAPTER 17

L EAVE," Mrs. Zimmermann said to Jonathan and Rose Rita. "Go. Back away. You'll know when to return. You'll know if you *should* return." She did not so much as glance at Rose Rita and Uncle Jonathan.

"No!" cried Rose Rita. But Uncle Jonathan firmly, gently pushed her into the car. He got into the driver's seat, started the engine, and with a screech of tires he recklessly backed away. The figures of Pele and Mrs. Zimmermann became two silhouettes sketched in orange and purple on the dark screen of night, circling each other. Flames flashed and leaped. Behind them, the Hawaii House lay bathed in unearthly colors, glowing and shimmering with a drifting net made up of all the hues of the rainbow.

In that wild, weird light, Rose Rita glimpsed movement. "Up there, in the tower! That's Lewis!"

Uncle Jonathan jammed his foot on the brake, and the big car lurched to a stop. "What's he doing?"

"I can't see!"

Rose Rita wanted to climb out of the car, to go running to help her friend. She realized with a pang that she couldn't do it. An army had grown out of the ground, or had formed from the air like fog. Gray in the darkness, all wearing crested helmets, all carrying spears, they stood in a grim line, shoulder to shoulder. They did not move, but held their ground like guards determined not to let anyone pass. Rose Rita could see right through them. The battle between Pele and Mrs. Zimmermann still raged. The house still writhed in quivering waves of light, as if it lay on the bottom of the sea.

But between the car and the house stood the gray warriors. Rose Rita knew she and Uncle Jonathan had no hope of getting past them. This was the army her grandfather had warned them about.

They were the Marching Dead.

Lewis emerged on the platform, feeling the chilling caress of cold night air. He had dragged himself out of the bedroom and up the tower stair. This night did not hold the killing cold of the one that had frozen old Abediah, but for someone wearing only cotton pajamas, it was bad enough.

A man stood at the railing that ran waist-high around the platform. He wore a long blue coat and a hat that looked a bit like a short top hat. His transparent hands gripped the rail, and he stared out at what was happening in the front yard. His face turned toward Lewis, and Abediah Chadwick's ghost spoke.

"A foul night, Mr. Barnavelt." Like the princess' voice, this one came not from the unmoving lips of the spirit, but simply formed in Lewis's mind. "Ye have a goodly crew, but who can stand against that island witch?"

"Captain Chadwick," said Lewis between chattering teeth.

"Aye. That was my name, while I walked the earth a living man."

"They didn't get her," Lewis said.

The ghost turned its face from him. "Aye, lad, that I know. Her spirit is confined to her room, and mine is locked here, because of Pele's curse. We are so close and yet never to be completely reunited, not so long as Pele's hatred endures. And a spirit can hold enough hate to last for all eternity."

"What can I do?"

"Leave this place. Leave us to unending misery. Oh, for a vessel that could sail the skies! For a swift ship upon the waves of the clouds, and a good deck beneath my boots! I had such a one, my schooner *Sword,* but she is driftwood and rust these many years."

Lights flashed down below, and Lewis craned to see what was happening. He gawped at the sight of Mrs. Zimmermann, dressed in wind-whipped purple robes, standing inside a circle of purple flames, holding her own against Pele, tall and imperious in her own circle of orange-red fire. They were chanting, taking turns back and forth. Lewis could not hear what they were saying, but it seemed a furious contest of wills.

"The tooth anchors Pele here."

"What?" Lewis spun toward the ghostly figure of the old sea captain. He was fading away, melting into the cold night air. Lewis threw himself into the stairwell, tore down to the top landing, and through the door of Makalani's room. The lurid red light had vanished, but the overhead bulbs were still on. Lewis knelt by the window and ran his fingers over the sill. He found a hole—a hole plugged by something hard and oval. If he only had something to pry with, he thought. He rushed to the stepladder and saw lying next to the can of paint a flat-head screwdriver. Lewis grabbed it, ran back to the window, and started to work on the plugged hole. He put the blade against the top of the plug and pounded the handle of the screwdriver with the heel of his left hand. Ouch! Once—twice—three times, and the screwdriver blade sank down as the plug gave way and clicked on the floor. Lewis grabbed it at once.

He held the broken shank of a shark's tooth. It

had been part of the club that Abediah Chadwick had swung at the ghostly army. Now Lewis grabbed his shoes, pulled them onto his feet, and hurtled down the stairs with the laces flapping. He nearly screamed out loud at the middle landing, where the light burned. Something was creeping toward him from the darkness below!

Then the shadowy form spoke: "L-L-Lewis? Muh-my m-mom and duh-d-dad w-won't w-wake up!"

"David! Stick with me!"

Lewis turned on the lights in the parlor. It didn't matter if he turned on every light and lamp in the house, if he screeched and screamed or sang "My Darling Clementine" at the top of his lungs, if the Kellers were under some kind of spell, and he thought they were. Lewis grabbed something from the shelf and then ordered, "Come on! Don't be afraid!"

The two boys pounded back up the stairs. Lewis didn't know what he was doing. All he could hold on to was a crazy, wild hope.

Pele challenged: "It can swim, it lies on the sand, you can hold it in your hand, it is round, it is small, but it stands more than a man's house tall!" She suddenly stood in the middle of swirling scarlet flames, and they rolled upward.

Mrs. Zimmermann felt the scorching heat on her face, but she did not give ground. "That is an easy one. A coconut! For a coconut is a seed that floats, that finds its way to land, and then grows into a tall tree. And now answer me this, if you can: This canoe holds a lowly traveler. Across a dry sea he rows with four short paddles. What is it?"

The contest of wits was as old as the oldest wizardry. No blinding flashes, no explosions or stabs of lightning. Just the quick thrust and parry of riddle and answer. Mrs. Zimmermann had thought of something as far from the islands of the Pacific as she could, hoping that the question would stump Pele. But the fiery spirit shook her head. "Ah, you try to be clever. But what rows itself across a desert but a tortoise?" She threw back her head and laughed. Billows of steam rose in the night air, tinted by the flames that burned around her.

Mrs. Zimmermann nodded, tilting her head. Was she crazy, or was Pele *enjoying* this? Mrs. Zimmermann tried to concentrate as the next challenge came: "I sail in a sea of deepest blue; when you sleep, I watch you; I sail to reach a golden shore, and when I reach it, I am no more!"

Mrs. Zimmermann bit her lip. She knew hundreds of old puzzles, but none were from Hawaii. As if sensing her indecision, Pele lifted the war club in a menacing way, and the flames around her flared so hot that Mrs. Zimmermann had to force herself to hold her ground. The rules were clear: If she failed to answer or she stepped back from her foe, she would lose her life. "You cannot answer, old woman?"

"A star sails the night sky," said Mrs. Zimmermann in a firm voice. "And when it reaches the shores of dawn, it fades."

Pele lowered her weapon. In a grudging tone, she said, "It is long since I met one like you, woman of the dry land."

Mrs. Zimmermann bowed. "And I have never met your like, spirit of the volcano."

"But only one of us can win."

Mrs. Zimmermann did not answer. She was desperately trying to think up a riddle that would stump Pele. The spirit's fury was barely contained. If she won the contest, Pele's anger would strike the house and everything around it in a burst of real fire, fire that would burn, fire that would kill.

And Lewis was still in that house.

"Captain!" Lewis stumbled out onto the platform. "Here!"

Carefully, as if he held a baby animal, Lewis set down the thing he had carried up from the parlor: a ship in a bottle, a trim, two-masted schooner named *Sword*. Behind Lewis, David gasped. As Lewis backed away, as he sat and hastily tied his shoes, a glowing form took shape above the ship in the bottle. "Such a sweet craft!" The captain's words rang in Lewis's mind. He didn't know whether David could hear it or not, but he didn't have time to find out.

Lewis held up the broken shark's tooth. "Can we use this?"

The captain's sea-blue eyes flashed. "Aye! That is a point from the war club given me by a mighty warrior on Maui. The spirit warriors cannot face it. Beware, though, that it does not fall into the hands of Pele! If you had the whole of it, you might be able to banish even her—"

"Stay here," gasped Lewis, so busy in his thoughts that he couldn't even be afraid. "David! You come with me!"

Down the steps, and Lewis threw the front door open. To their left, Mrs. Zimmermann and Pele circled each other, their voices alternating, rising, falling, challenging. Both of them were surrounded by flames, crimson ones rising around Pele, purple ones flickering from Mrs. Zimmermann's wand. Past the two women, the Marching Dead stood shoulder to shoulder like a ghostly fence surrounding the house. "Come on," Lewis said. He led the way across the lawn, and then he could see Uncle Jonathan and Rose Rita standing yards distant, helplessly watching. He heard his uncle call his name.

Lewis held the shark's tooth out ahead of him. Closing his eyes, he touched one of the warriors. A jolt, like electricity, throbbed through Lewis's arm, nearly knocking him backward. He heard David's cry of amazement and opened his eyes. The ghostly form had dissolved into mist. With his free hand,

Lewis shoved David forward. David stumbled, went sprawling, but burst through the ghostly barrier an eye-blink before the guards on either side of the gap stepped to seal it. Pele shrieked in anger. Uncle Jonathan and Rose Rita were in the distance, yelling to David.

Lewis had no time. He shouted, "David! My room, the top desk drawer, in an old aspirin bottle! Looks like an arrowhead! Bring it back, and hurry!"

He retreated, holding the broken tooth before him. Mrs. Zimmermann's angry voice lashed out: "Pele! If you turn away from me, I claim victory!"

Pele stood enveloped in flames. "I am immortal! What is time to me? I shall finish you, old woman, and then take all your spirits!"

The warriors were closing in. Lewis backed up the front steps, ran into the parlor, fought a terrible stitch in his side as he climbed those steps again.

On the platform, Abediah Chadwick looked almost solid. "Captain! Can we hold out?"

"Aye, Mr. Barnavelt!" Lewis shivered. The man's fierce expression was that of an eagle, or that of a lion, unbeaten and unbeatable. Pele could not have defeated this man. She could only kill him.

The Muggins Simoon screeched to a stop in front of the Barnavelt house, and three figures spilled out of it and rushed inside. "Hurry," urged Uncle Jonathan. "I can't stand the thought of leaving Florence and Lewis to hold off those horrors alone!"

Rose Rita trembled. She hated to feel helpless. They all hurried to Lewis's bedroom, and David yanked the desk drawer open. He rummaged, throwing odds and ends onto the floor: a Boy Scout knife, a British shilling piece, pencils, old keys, and all the other junk that Lewis had tossed in over the years. With a cry of "H-here it is!" David held up a St. Joseph's aspirin bottle. Something in it rattled.

Uncle Jonathan took it from him, unscrewed the top, and shook a white pointed something into his palm. "This is it?"

"I remember that!" exclaimed Rose Rita. "It's an arrowhead that I found at the Hawaii House a long time ago!"

"Not an arrowhead," said Uncle Jonathan. "This is a tooth."

"Kuh-quick," begged David. "Wuh-we've g-got to g-get b-back."

"Right you are. Come on, everyone!"

Rose Rita held on as the car lurched and roared its way through the night. It seemed to her that only a few moments had passed, but when Uncle Jonathan stomped on the brakes and the big old car slid to a stop, things looked different. Mrs. Zimmermann and Pele still faced each other. Now, though, Mrs. Zimmermann leaned on her staff as if she were growing weary. And the Marching Dead had gone.

A thin voice cried out from the platform in the tower: "Uncle Jonathan! Don't come in the house! The ghosts are inside!"

"They can't take David's family!" shouted Mrs. Zimmermann. "Not as long as I hold off Pele!"

"But how long can you do that, old woman?" The voice of the spirit was haughty and proud.

"I've got it, Lewis!" called Uncle Jonathan.

Rose Rita couldn't understand what Lewis was doing. He appeared to be conversing with someone she couldn't see. Then he yelled down, "I have to have it, Uncle Jonathan! But I can't get down, and you can't come up the stairs!"

"Oh, I can't, can't I?" snarled Uncle Jonathan. He held out his cane. "Grab on to this, David and Rose Rita! Hold tight and close your eyes if you want to. Just don't let go!"

Rose Rita seized the cane, her hand just below David's. In the next moment, Uncle Jonathan bellowed, *"Volans!"*

Rose Rita felt the breath catch in her chest. The cane had responded. It yanked them upward.

The three of them rose from the earth and flew through the air.

CHAPTER 18

L EWIS HAD NEVER SEEN anything as wonderful as Uncle Jonathan, Rose Rita, and David sailing from the earth up, up to the tower. They arched over the rail, and, one, two, three, they touched down. "Lewis!" gasped Uncle Jonathan. "What's happened? What does that tooth mean?"

"It has some kind of power," replied Lewis. "Did you find it?"

Uncle Jonathan fumbled in his vest pocket and took out the rattling aspirin bottle. He handed it to Lewis, and Lewis shook the broken tip of the tooth into his palm. He fitted the base to it, and it made a perfect match. "Can you—glue this together? Can you make it whole?"

"No sooner said than done," growled Uncle Jonathan. He raised his cane and intoned a Latin phrase that Lewis mentally translated as "Let the broken be healed!" A thin blue ray, as fine as a spiderweb, shot from the crystal orb on his cane and touched the two jagged pieces of tooth. Lewis felt them pulsate on his palm. A flash of blue light, and he held a complete tooth, with not even a hairline fracture.

"W-w-wow," said David, who still looked shaky after his flight through the air.

"Now the ship," said Lewis, pointing toward the ship model in the bottle. "Uncle Jonathan, Captain Chadwick here—"

"They can't see me," intoned the ghost.

"What?" asked Uncle Jonathan and Rose Rita in unison. David backed away, his eyes wide.

"He's here, his ghost is here." The words tumbled out of Lewis. He felt there wasn't much time. "Listen, he needs for this ship to be a real ship, or at least a real ghostly ship. Uncle Jonathan, can you—"

"Tall order," said Uncle Jonathan. "Stand back, everyone!" He stood over the model, waving his wand and murmuring something, his eyes closed. From below them, Lewis heard Pele's angry voice rising, speaking raging words in a language he did not know.

Then the model ship began to grow. Lewis stepped back in alarm, expecting the bottle to shatter. But the little model was still there. What was swelling up in the night air was a transparent illusion, like the ghost of a ship. Chadwick shouted out, "That's my craft! Aye, there be fine magic here!"

As the ghost ship grew, the breeze caught the insubstantial sails, puffing them out, and by the time the model schooner was the size of a rowboat, it had begun to float out into the night, passing through the rail as if it were no more than a wisp of mist. Captain Chadwick leaped aboard, and then the schooner was the size of a truck. In another instant it had become life-sized. "I see him now!" shouted Rose Rita. David whimpered.

"No!" The cry from below lashed like a whip. "You cannot escape me!"

David clapped his hands over his ears. "H-help!"

Captain Chadwick's ghost laughed, a defiant sound. He spun the ship's wheel, and the schooner banked in a curve as graceful as the elegant flight of a gull. The craft's bow dipped, and the vessel plunged right through the roof of the house. An instant later, it emerged from the wall below. And now a second figure stood beside Abediah Chadwick at the wheel. Princess Makalani embraced her husband.

"I will call the Marching Dead!" shrieked Pele, swelling in her rage.

"No," said Mrs. Zimmermann firmly. "You have not defeated me."

Red flame rolled off the angry spirit. "Nor have you defeated me!"

"It's a tie!" bellowed Uncle Jonathan.

Mrs. Zimmermann gestured with an imperious arm. Lewis felt a wave of silence. He didn't dare try to speak. He hardly dared to breathe. Everything in the world had come to some sort of perilous balance. One hair out of place now, and it would all crash down.

"Look at the princess," said Mrs. Zimmermann softly. "You could not claim her. Death itself could not break the bond of love she felt with her husband. She is not yours, Pele. She belongs only to herself. Admit that."

Pele rumbled, and dark smoke boiled up. It was going wrong.

"Ahoy!" shouted Captain Chadwick. "If it pleases you, I will sail this craft to the islands. There my love and I will find our final reward. What do I care if I am here or there? Where she stands beside me, there heaven is! You have your pearl, and you have the enchanted war club. Your treasures are safe. Let us keep our own!"

"No!" Pele brandished the club. "It is no longer as it was! Even for the loss of a single tooth, you must pay!"

Lewis handed Rose Rita the shark tooth. For a moment she just looked at him. His mouth felt dry as a stone. "Remember how Skunky threw the pearl. I'd suggest a fastball," he managed.

With a look of determination, Rose Rita gripped

the tooth as if it were a stone she wanted to skim across a pond. She whipped a lightning sidearm pitch. Like the pearl that Skunky had thrown, the whirling tooth kindled. It trailed out a yellow streak of fire. Rose Rita had thrown the most perfect pitch of her life.

The white-hot spark struck the war club that Pele had raised above her head. With a flash of fire, the whole club exploded, leaving black dots dancing before Lewis's eyes.

He heard a clap of thunder that shook the entire house, though the night had been clear.

Pele . . . laughed.

Then the sound faded into the twittering of birds, hundreds of them. Lewis felt as though an enormous weight had lifted from his shoulders.

And in the east, like a tide swelling in an immense ocean, dawn rose and flooded the night sky, turning it a brilliant, clear, deep blue. Night fled before it, and the sun came up on a bright, crisp new day.

A week later, Uncle Jonathan, Lewis, Mrs. Zimmermann, and Rose Rita jounced along a concrete road in Bessie, Mrs. Zimmermann's purple car. "I understand that Pele went away and took the Dead Warrior Marching Society and Saturday Night Pinochle Club with her," grumbled Uncle Jonathan. "We've been over that. What I really want to know is did we win or lose?"

Mrs. Zimmermann turned the wheel as they passed a slowpoke old Studebaker. "I think everyone won, Brush Mush. I believe Pele released the souls of those poor servants who perished in the Hawaii House back in 1876, and that they have found their place in eternity. I'm sure that Captain Abediah Chadwick kept his word, and that he and Princess Makalani sailed away to Hawaii on the ship you conjured up. Nice bit of magic, by the way."

"Thank you, Haggy," returned Uncle Jonathan. "Just one of my basic illusion spells, but I suppose an illusion is solid enough for your average run-of-the-mill ghost. Tell me about the pearl and that whack-'em-on-the-head doojigger, though. What were they?"

"Sacred relics. Oh, don't ask me the details. I don't know, and Pele certainly didn't tell me. The pearl was the eye of an idol, maybe. The war club might have been consecrated to Pele after some great chief won a victory in battle with it. But they were *hers,* and that's the point. Returning them was the whole key. Poor Potsworth had exactly the right idea when he told the phantom army they could have the pearl and threw it to them. He surrendered the trophy of his own free will, you see, just as Rose Rita did when she made that excellent side-arm toss with the shark's tooth. When the two items turned into mystical fire, Pele got them back in some way and in some form. Without them, without actual solid

169

relics that had been dedicated to her, and her alone, Pele held no real claim to remain here. In the end, she accepted that the princess was not hers to command. I think that after all was said and done, even Pele had to admire the strength and the depth of human love."

"Mr. Chadwick had his own relic," put in Jonathan. "A sailor always thinks his ship has magic in its very canvas and wood."

"And Mr. Chadwick could reunite with the princess because he had the *Sword,*" said Rose Rita with a sigh.

Lewis rolled his eyes. Sometimes Rose Rita could sound positively mushy.

They had reached the outskirts of Ann Arbor, a university town. Mrs. Zimmermann turned up one street and down another, and at last they parked in front of a long red brick building.

"There he is!" shouted Rose Rita. "Hey, David!"

David and his parents had just emerged from the building. They waved and hurried over as everyone spilled out of Bessie. "Hello, hello," Mrs. Zimmermann said to the Kellers, who were all smiling and looking flustered. "What's the news?"

"G-g-great," David said. "The th-therapist s-says sh-she can help me learn not—" he swallowed. "Not to s-stutter. If I try hard. And I'm g-going to!"

Ernest Keller had his arm around his wife's waist. "Thank you so much," he said to Uncle Jonathan and Mrs. Zimmermann. "We could never have afforded treatment for David. But the university is willing do it for free. David will have sessions twice a week from the visiting therapist. I know this means a lot to him. To us all."

"How can we ever repay you for finding someone who could help David?" asked Mrs. Keller.

"Simple," boomed Uncle Jonathan. "Just let David ride back to New Zebedee with us, and we'll treat him to a banana split the likes of which few have ever seen!"

The Kellers agreed, and David scrambled into the backseat of Mrs. Zimmermann's car. "You didn't tell them anything about that night?" asked Lewis with some anxiety as soon as they had started toward home.

"N-no," David said. "Th-they w-wouldn't believe me anyway. All th-they know is th-that th-they g-got a really g-good night's s-sleep that n-night, and every other one s-since. B-but L-Lewis, your uncle's a m-magician! And Mrs. Z-Zimmermann is the b-bravest person I know!"

"And the smartest too," said Mrs. Zimmermann with a dry little laugh. "Lucky for me that I had learned the little tidbit about Pele. You know, to fox a vampire, you need to scatter about a bushel of rice in his way. He gets obsessed with picking up every single grain and can't chase you until it's done. My challenge worked the same way with Pele. Once she agreed to match me in the riddle contest, she had to stay in until one of us won, or until we both agreed to call it a draw. There are powerful rules that even ancient spirits must follow. She nearly stumped me on an easy one, though. I realized the answer was 'pineapple' just in time to save my wrinkled skin!"

"Shall I tell them the real news, your most purple majesty?" asked Jonathan.

With an amused chuckle, Mrs. Zimmermann said, "Go ahead."

Uncle Jonathan half turned in the front seat. "Well, we think that Pele has pulled up stakes and returned home for good. In fact, we're all but certain of that. No dreams of drums lately, right, David?"

David shook his head. "Nuh-not since th-that night," he said.

Uncle Jonathan gave a pleased nod. "But to make sure, we're going to take the little ship in a bottle to Pele's home—all of us. We plan to go next year, the very first day you kids are out for your summer break. Rose Rita's parents are thrilled that she'll have the chance to visit Hawaii, David's parents have agreed that I am not really a nut case and can serve as a good chaperone, and I know Lewis will like it once he gets over his fear of being seasick."

"Please," groaned Lewis, imagining a heaving sea and a tiny, tempest-tossed ship.

"Buck up, nephew! It will be a grand voyage to Hawaii and back on a comfortable modern ship," finished Uncle Jonathan. "We are going to visit Mount Kilauea, just to be sure that everything on the Pele front is as calm and peaceful as it should be. I will place the model of the *Sword* in a fine museum on the island. If I am not very much mistaken, that will seal the deal that old Abediah Chadwick made, and I hope that it will let the couple find eternal happiness together at last. I plan to buy myself a red and yellow and green and purple Hawaiian shirt and I will wear a grass skirt, plunk out a tune on the ukelele, and dance the hula on the beach at Waikiki. If Pele enjoys a good laugh, that should last her for a long time. And if any spirits should disagree and act up in an unpleasant way, I'm simply going to hand Rose Rita a baseball."

"And I'll give them the fastball," said Rose Rita. "High, hard, and inside!"

"Strike 'em out, champ!" cheered Lewis.

David chuckled at that, and Lewis felt good himself as the car rolled through a bright November day, heading back to New Zebedee and home.